THE ORACUS TEST

By Corrie Hathaway

To my best friend, Amiretty Lyne Bourke. Spleen on me.

CONTENTS

CHAPTER 1

The inductee uniform was not designed with comfort in mind. I tugged at the stiff fabric jutting from my shoulders, trying to loosen the seams pinching my armpits. It didn't take a Seer to foretell that I'd take this off the moment the ceremony was over.

"Tallie?" Mom poked her head through my partially open bedroom door. "We have to leave in five minutes if we want to be on time."

I could have spent the next five minutes arranging intestines on the floor to let her know if we would be late. I wouldn't get access to intrinsic predictions until after the ceremony. After I crossed the threshold into the Oracus, claiming my place as a Seer, I would gain the power to see the future unfold without requiring pieces of dead animals or any other predictive material.

That was one of the main reasons I looked forward to my time in the Oracus. That and my parents would be cemented in their Elite status, despite providing the nation with one measly child. When I became a Seer, it would be enough. I would finally be enough.

"I don't need five minutes," I told her, concentrating on not fussing with the damnable shoulder drapes. "We can leave right now."

She sighed in relief. "Aiden!" she called down the hallway for Dad. "It's time!"

Mom stepped fully into my room and wrapped me in a hug that turned awkward in a hurry. She leaned back to pat the tops and sides of the shoulder drapes, frowning at them.

"These certainly weren't designed with hugging in mind," she said, then settled for dropping a quick, dry kiss on my forehead.

Two minutes later, Mom, Dad, and I were in the car. Once I was Foretold and started my education in the assisted forms of divination, the directorate allowed them vehicle access. Ours was small, electric, and white. Also very old. The battery was new, but the body had been manufactured before the separation of the states.

A high-pitched tone sounded from the speakers, starting out soft and rapidly increasing to a blare.

"Pedestrian disturbance on Route Twenty-Three," an announcer droned. "All induction attendees take alternate routes."

The radio fell silent—its default mode. Radios in our car and house were always on, in case of an official announcement.

Mom sighed. "Tallie, this is why I don't want you around them. These people are unpredictable."

"Dangerous, really," Dad said. "Imagine if they had access to one of these." He slapped the dashboard. "They'd be mowing each other down. No foresight or thought for consequence."

I pressed my cheek to the window, letting the shoulder drapes dig into my skin to the point of pain. A reminder not to contradict my parents about the Pedestrians. Dad liked to talk above them. It wasn't like he could predict the future or do anything but cook a good meal.

Mom drove a circuitous route that forced us to travel through neighborhoods I hadn't set foot in for three years. The houses were smaller and close together. Weeds sprouted from cracked, empty driveways that were obsolete after the wars. Almost every house had a vegetable garden, some with a chicken coop or even a goat pen. The animals made each stuffy block more crowded.

Both sets of shoulders in the front seat stiffened. They'd be uncomfortable until we passed the area. This was the site of my "teenage rebellion," as they called it, but only in hushed tones when they thought I couldn't hear, as though I'd realize I was only eighteen and had another year and a half of being a teenager and could do it again.

I craned my neck to spy the top of a rusted, metal tower. The towers hovered over the houses every five blocks; relics of attempts to reclaim cellular phone service. Whatever that was like.

In a blur, something struck my window. I shrieked and reared back, ramming an unyielding shoulder drape into the back of my seat. More balloons struck the windshield and sides of the car. They burst on impact, splattering loose, oozing mud.

How did anyone in this neighborhood get *balloons*?

"If I wouldn't get a face full of dirt by opening the window, I'd let those kids have it," Dad said, turning an unnatural shade of red.

"They can't quite help themselves, can they?" Mom replied, soothing and scorning in tandem as she pressed on the gas a little harder.

Though my heart hammered, I peered through the streaks of brown on my window, wanting to see the pranksters. A few unfamiliar faces laughed our way, nudging each other in victory behind a small wooden … trebuchet? What kind of person had the time to build a working model of historical weaponry? I couldn't remember having the time or inclination to build anything since I was Foretold. Aside from my stolen time with … I shook my head. It hurt to remember.

A pair of deep-set blue eyes stood out from the rest. I didn't think I was visible behind the glass, between the drips, but his mischievous grin faltered as he stared into my window.

Vance.

My heart stuttered to a halt. There was no way he recognized me, but I could never be mistaken about him.

The presence of balloons made more sense. He and his crew made a habit of exploring run-down, abandoned buildings, at least during the year I'd known them. They'd dragged me to half-demolished places that were never reconstructed after the wars, that sometimes contained relics from a more prosperous past. It was exciting at the time, but the past three years had dulled the memory of adventure and rebellion. I'd been a fool.

Oblivious to my turmoil, my parents dropped me off at the front lawn of the Oracus.

"We knew you'd make it, our determined girl," Mom said.

"I wonder if they'll acknowledge high achievers," Dad mused, drumming his fingers on top of the steering wheel. "Or the one high achiever. Right, Tallie girl?"

I smiled in that practiced way I had for years. I was the perfect student. The perfect future Seer. Everyone expected me to excel because that was what I always did. It left no room for anything else.

The Oracus lawn was almost unrecognizable. Rows of folding chairs covered its pristine grass, leaving a narrow aisle down the middle that led to the Oracus' entry gate. Almost every chair was occupied; the first two rows full of my classmates. From the third row all the way to the back, each attendant held a single balloon. Latex products were almost nonexistent, but gaining new Seers was a cause for celebration.

I swallowed, my mouth suddenly dry, and tried one last time to adjust my shoulder drapes into a semblance of comfort. Futility in the key of ceremonial fashion.

A tight smile between braided pigtails caught my eye in the front row of seats. Bryla, one of my school friends, waved to me and patted the empty seat next to her. I clenched and unclenched my fists one time each. This was it. I made my way down the aisle to the seat Bryla saved for me.

"I thought you were going to be late," she said.

"They predicted a parade interruption, so we had to go through a different neighborhood. Then some Pedestrians drenched the car in mud. We stopped to clear the windows." I shrugged, hoping she wouldn't ask any follow-up questions. My parents tried hard to keep my "teenage rebellion" in the past and out of anyone's knowledge.

Thankfully, Maynor Raunheim, Steward of the Oracus, stepped up to the microphone at the front of the seating area. He was a broad man: broad shoulders, broad nose, broad ambitions. He began the ceremony without warning, "Welcome, esteemed Elites, future Seers, and supporters,"

I hoped my parents reached their seats on time, but they could always sneak into the back row. All eyes would be on the new Seers of the nation. After entering the Oracus today, the public would rarely see us, even after two months when we were fit for full service.

"The early twenty-first century was marked by war between the states until peace was negotiated via separation into individual nations," Maynor said, his high-pitched voice not given any favors by the microphone or speaker system. "In the past fourteen years, Michigan has risen above its neighbors in prosperity and success. It's no coincidence that this marks the fourteenth year of the Oracus. Where others have shunned the predictive capabilities that arose from years of chemical and biological warfare, Michigan has recognized their value."

My throat bulged as I fought back a yawn. Without moving my head, I snuck a peek to the right. Brayla sat forward in her chair, eyes wide and rapt. I tried to mimic my friend, pretending I hadn't heard this same speech when I attended entrance ceremonies every year since I'd been Foretold.

"Seerdom is essential in the continued prosperity of our nation. With each new Seer, we gain access to future events in more locations we previously were not staffed to monitor. With each prediction, we can prepare for all eventualities, protecting against our enemies and anticipating the needs of our citizens. Director Hooper sends his fondest regards to our newest, our best, and our brightest. Our new Seers. I will call them forward, one at a time, to enter the gate."

Maynor began listing names, allowing only a few seconds in between. Future forbid anyone tripped and fell, breaking the even chain of bodies disappearing through the gate. If that happened, Maynor would probably keep listing the names, letting the others tromp over the fallen Seer on their way to the gate. The process appeared that mechanized.

Then he said it.

"Natalie Kowalczyk."

Fearing I would miss my three-second window, I stood a little too fast and dipped a toe into the waters of dizziness. Forcing myself into steady body and vision, I moved forward, as automated as the rest, with my eyes trained on the gate. Toward a year of focus on the future, then a lifetime of service. A duty the nation needed me to perform. The importance of the task always on my mind. The burden of being skilled at divination, so the others looked to me to be first to complete my predictions, to be most accurate, every time.

Knowing that if I performed at anything less than perfection, *everyone* would notice, remember, and reference it in perpetuity. There would be concerns and sneers and *assessments*.

Black spots appeared at the sides of my vision. Not now. I couldn't give in to the stress that threatened to derail me. Breathing deeply, clenching one fist, then the other, I reached the glazed panels on either side of the gate and stepped through.

At least, I tried to step through. My foot ricocheted off the air.

Steadying myself, I tried again, sticking my head forward. I gasped when my neck snapped backward, taking my head and upper body with it. I couldn't get in.

The black spots increased and crowded their way into the center of my vision. Sweat beaded at my temples. I lifted both arms and shoved at the empty air between the gate panels, but it was as if there was an invisible blockade.

"Tallie, what are you doing?" Bryla hissed from behind me. "Go!"

I tried to obey, pressing my hands forward and putting my shoulders into it. I planted my feet on the ground and shoved for all I was worth. But I was not passing through the gate.

A wave of murmurs washed through the crowd. Maynor's voice no longer announced a stream of names. My shoulders jolted at the sharp sound of a balloon popping, worsening the pinch of fabric at my armpits. I couldn't turn around. It was too much.

A hand clamped my shoulder but removed itself immediately. I supposed I had the shoulder drapes to thank for that.

Maynor stepped into my narrowing field of vision. "There must be some malfunction in the gate," he muttered, two deep lines forming in the center of his forehead like someone had carved the number eleven there. "Unheard of. Where are the technicians when you need them? Worthless Pedestrians." Blathering on, he examined the side panels. Pausing to give me a hard look, he stepped through the gate himself. He passed through, then came back outside. He ran his tongue over his upper lip, first in one direction, then the other, and wrung his hands together. "Natalie, step aside here next to me. Bryla, go ahead. We'll see if it works for the rest of you."

If I blinked, the welling tears would take that as permission to fall. I didn't need the additional humiliation. Keeping my eyes wide open and downcast, I shuffled to the side.

As soon as I cleared the path, Bryla walked past, hesitating only once in her stride. I looked up, needing to know if the gate malfunctioned, or if it was just me.

My friend passed through without a hitch, disappearing into the unknown of the Oracus. She hadn't looked back.

Maynor tsked once, then prodded me forward to try again.

My chest burned, needing this to work. I had to be let through. This was impossible.

I closed my eyes and stepped forward with more force than wisdom.

My whole body bounced backward from the gate. I stumbled at the momentum, tipped back, and landed on my butt on the stage.

It had rejected me. This had never happened in the history of Seers and the Oracus.

The gates had sensors that allowed only Seers, the Steward, and certain high-level officials inside. But a Seer had foretold my entrance. My talent was undeniable. I had worked endlessly to stay at the top of my class for years, and I should have been inside. I was supposed to be inside, finally fulfilling my purpose.

Hot tears of humiliation spilled down my cheeks, no matter how I wished they wouldn't. Maynor gripped my elbow and pulled me to standing. His thick fingers dug in painfully as he guided me to the side and behind him, partially shielded from the audience's view.

"We'll sort this out later. Continuing on. Nicholas Mitchell," he said and listed the rest of the names.

Each person walked through the gate with ease until the last person disappeared inside. Once through the gate, no outsider could see you. The inner Oracus was a mystery to the unprivileged.

That group included me.

A hush fell over the audience. Normally, there would be applause.

A small brass band stood at uneasy attention behind the seats until Maynor mimed the arm movements of a conductor. A trumpet or two squeaked wrong notes in the awkward atmosphere, but the rest of the jaunty music absorbed the errors and heralded the end of the ceremony.

Audience members eyed each other in muted discomfort as they waved their balloons over their heads in time to the music. The new Seers had been accepted into the Oracus to receive their final training.

Where did that leave me?

CHAPTER 2

"Tallie!" Mom called my name from where she stood behind the row of chairs, restrained in Dad's arms. The skins of their broken balloons lay at their feet.

Two men with shaved heads, wearing matching gray suits led me in the opposite direction toward a waiting car. They wore no identification but held the official air of the director's guard. There was no point in resisting. I didn't think being denied entry to the Oracus was a jailable offense, just a public embarrassment that would last a lifetime. If anything, they would ensure I made it home safely.

I waved once to my parents, unable to make eye contact. All their hopes for me, and their source of pride, vanished in a thirty-minute ceremony. A lecture awaited me at home. It was sure to feature the words *disappointment* and *out of character* at least a dozen times.

One of the suited men opened the rear door of the sleek silver car and waited for me to enter and buckle myself before closing me in. The men took their seats in the front and drove away.

The only thing they'd said to me was "Come with us" when the fanfare had ended.

Maybe I should have asked questions. If I were in the Oracus, I would have instant knowledge of certain events, and wouldn't be sitting here wondering, like a Pedestrian fool. The embarrassment burned too hot for me to ask what would happen next. By all rights, I should've known.

The trip took countless turns—I swore they drove in circles—before we stopped in front of a three-story, rectangular brick home. A city block distanced it from its neighbors in either direction. A man opened my door and ushered me outside. Wordlessly, both men led me past the front door of the home and around to a second door on the side of the building. I was almost willing to bear my shame by asking where I was and what would happen, but there was the vague impression I wouldn't be given a choice. Maybe knowing what the future held wasn't all it claimed to be.

We entered the house after a rhythmic series of knocks. A professionally dressed woman met us inside. She gave me an up-and-down perusal, her lips pursed in distaste, then she turned on her heel to stride deeper into the home.

Portraits of Director Hooper and his family hung along the hallway. Layers of wooden molding added an artistic flair to the walls, and a mandala-patterned rug absorbed the sound of the woman's steps.

Did any of these people talk? Maybe there were pay cuts for each sound they made while on duty.

Finally, we stopped at a set of double doors. Another series of knocks, with a different rhythm than the first, then the woman opened both doors to reveal a minimalistic office. Sparse furnishings exaggerated the enormity of the room. A desk hugged the far wall; the man behind it was all the decoration needed.

Director Hooper. The Foretold leader of Michigan.

He stood from his desk chair and smiled, painting a picture of relaxed confidence in his khaki pants and dress shirt with the sleeves rolled up past his forearms.

"Please, come in," he said.

At least *he* could talk.

I hesitated, wanting one of the official people to enter the room first, but they all turned to stare at me. I considered apologizing but couldn't muster the ability. After I walked a few paces into the room, the double doors closed with a resounding thud behind me. With a gasp, I twirled to look. None of them had entered the room, leaving me alone with the director.

If my future hadn't just crumbled in front of a hundred witnesses, I might have giggled with nerves at this unexpected turn of events. That thought alone was enough to quell any levity. My entire future would be full of unexpected events.

The director walked around to the front of his desk, leaning his hips back against it and crossing his arms over his chest. He looked a lot younger in person, even with his dark hair slicked straight back. I had overheard my mom talking with a neighbor after the Seers foretold his Presidency. She had called him a fox, which had made me gag. Now, in person, I kind of saw what she meant—not for me, but in terms of general attractiveness.

He sighed heavily. "This is a tragedy."

I nodded in complete agreement. But what could my personal struggles mean to him?

"You understand we need a guarantee of the utmost discretion from you."

"I'm sorry," I said slowly, my voice coming out croaky. "I don't understand. Discretion about what?"

His eyes narrowed as he stood straight, like he practiced intimidation in the mirror every morning. "Our nation's Seers are infallible. That fact is the very frame of our nation. The Seer who foretold your entry to the Oracus was not," he swallowed with a grimace, "mistaken. That could not be true. Either you sabotaged the process or did not pass muster. It was a failure of yours, not of the Seer's prediction."

I didn't know what to say. Maybe I should have apologized again, told him I'd try harder next time. That was what I'd done with authority figures my whole life, aside from my "teenage rebellion" years. And look where that got me. I'd tried my hardest every day since, but I hadn't lived up to my future.

"For the attendees, we have provided an incentive for their silence. Rumors of what transpired will be dismissed as conspiracy or hearsay. You will quietly disappear into the background with Pedestrians, never to draw attention for the rest of your life."

"Do my parents—"

"Your parents will relocate to a city where their neighbors won't know they had a daughter."

Had. He said *had* a daughter.

"But where will I—"

He interrupted me again, anticipating my questions easily enough that I wondered if he possessed Seer talent.

"You will live in an apprentice dormitory with the other Pedestrians of your age group, telling the others you couldn't cut life as a Seer. Choose a path for a craft and live an unremarkable life, beginning now."

"But I—"

"Guards," Director Hooper said.

The double doors opened, revealing the two men in suits. They escorted me out of the office, down the hallway, out the side door, and into the car before I had a chance to fully comprehend anything.

"Do you need my address?" I asked the driver. "So I can go home to pack?"

Neither of them answered.

I settled back into my seat, losing myself in thoughts of what I could say to my parents and what they would say to me. Would they scold me? Or pretend it was okay when it so obviously wasn't? They might even be relieved to move away for my … apprenticeship. My eyes turned watery at the thought.

The houses we passed began to look familiar—not like those from my neighborhood, but the houses I used to visit with my old friends. I spotted clods of mud on the street, from an hour or two earlier. This was Vance's neighborhood.

The car pulled to a stop in front of a plain box of a building, three stories high, with multiple narrow windows running along the sides in rows. An apprentice dormitory—somewhere Pedestrians could stay while they learned a craft to make a living and serve the nation.

If either man demanded I list the options for a craft, I doubted I could name even one, aside from my dad's. My future was blank, empty, unknowable.

"Wait—do my parents know where I am?" I asked as a sudden panic seized my chest. "Will they come see me before they move?"

The man in the passenger seat stared at the driver for a moment before turning his head to look at me. "No. They're gone already. They packed one box of your belongings, as instructed, which you'll find in your dormitory."

If I thought I'd used all my tears up at the ceremony, I was wrong. No matter how much I dreaded my parents' reaction to my failure, I needed to see them to say goodbye and apologize. Would I ever get the chance? I hadn't even been able to hug my mom properly that morning.

My shoulders shook under their oppressive fabric as tears overtook me. I lifted the end of a sleeve to wipe my eyes and blow my nose, planning to throw the garment in the trash as soon as possible. I couldn't show up at the dormitory with a runny nose and wet eyes. The Pedestrians wouldn't give me any kind of warm welcome. Not in this outfit.

The answer from the passenger seat had been a lone, meager act of kindness. They ushered me from the car, pointed me toward the door to the building, then drove away. In silence, go figure.

CHAPTER 3

"Natalie Kowalczyk," I said for the second time to the woman behind the desk. "K-O-W-A—"

"Oh, yes, you were the late addition. That explains why you aren't on my list. A very silent man in a," she paused and fanned her face, "very well-fitting suit brought your information and belongings not twenty minutes ago."

They moved fast.

I tried to conjure a smile for the woman, but it must have failed. Her eyebrows raised and pinched together, and she bustled around the desk to stand in front of me, placing a hand on my shoulder. She removed it immediately.

"My, that fabric is unpleasant to touch."

Tell me about it.

"You are on the top floor, room three fourteen. Your belongings are already present, as is your roommate for now. Once crafts are chosen, that will change. Be in the basement meeting hall at nine tomorrow morning for more information on apprentice positions."

I nodded through each detail, hoping I could retain them. A replay of my failure to enter the Oracus gate bogged down my mind. Everything had gone so wrong. My life was unrecognizable from this morning. I just hoped no one would know me here. My personal shame was enough; I didn't need others recognizing what I was capable of but couldn't achieve.

The shoulder drapes had to go.

I thanked the woman and took the stairs two at a time for the first flight until she was out of view. On the third floor, a hallway stretched in both directions, with doors close enough together to assume the rooms were small. Nothing indicated what direction the room numbers went, so I chose left at random.

So many actions and decisions would be random when they should have been Foretold.

The room numbers decreased as I walked. Three zero six. Three zero four. I turned around to search the other end of the hallway when a voice from the past froze me in place.

"Tallie. What is this? Some kind of Seer hazing? Slum it with the Pedestrians?"

Vance.

Thawing slowly, I turned around and was struck by the force of his eyes boring into mine. That expression—it bordered on anger, or at least resentment. Then he softened, his lips formed a smile, and I didn't know what to think. It had been years. His thick auburn hair was shaggier than it used to be, disheveled on top of his head. He'd grown into the diamond shape of his face. It no longer looked too angular on a skinny frame. That skinny frame was history, too.

He wore a plaid shirt, sleeves rolled just under his elbows. Soft-looking jeans and tan work boots completed the look, and I was a goner all over again. I ran a quick finger under each eye, hoping there was no lingering evidence of my earlier tears.

"Right," he said, after waiting through my silence. "Too good to talk to any of us, still. Finish up whatever it is you're doing here and get lost. None of the others will be glad to see you."

With his cold stare underscoring his words, I assumed the others would be downright hostile. I needed to say something. Anything.

A door opened, revealing a tall, slender girl with straight black hair and plump lips.

"Vance," she crooned. "I thought I heard you out here still. Did you want to come back in to say goodbye one more time?"

The girl ignored me with ease. Either that, or I had turned invisible.

"Sorry, Em. Ran into someone who is obviously lost." He separated each word, forming them into sharp points in his mouth.

She grabbed his hand and placed it on her hip, forcing him to turn her way as she stepped forward to kiss him.

The bottom fell out of my stomach, and I staggered backward. He had never replied to my letter three years ago. That had been answer enough. He didn't need to make out with some beauty queen in front of me to drive home the point.

I turned from the grotesque scene and ran. My vision tunneled until I reached the end of the hallway. I looked to my left. Three fifteen. I looked to my right. Three fourteen.

I fumbled with the handle, pushed the door open, and stumbled into the room after it.

Regaining my balance, I slammed the door, locked the knob, slid in the chain, then leaned my back against it, panting and trying not to cry for the millionth time that day.

"Uh, hi?" a husky female voice asked.

I blinked away the budding tears and tried to focus on whoever it was. Presumably, my new roommate.

"Sorry, just—sorry, give me a second." I pressed the heels of my hands against my eyes, wishing like hell I had a handful of sticks, even pig intestines. I would give anything to know if my future held just *one thing* to look forward to.

"It's cool," she said after a brief pause.

Steadying myself with a deep breath, I moved my hands to focus on my roommate, who had to be less than impressed with her current living situation, i.e., me.

She had blonde hair in an asymmetrical bob, cast partially over one eye. She bent over a tattered notebook, writing in cramped letters. Swiping her hair away from her face, she revealed smudges of black ink that covered the side of her hand.

"Sorry," I started to say.

"You apologized twice already. No need."

Oh. Okay. I pinched my lower lip between my teeth, willing my mouth to avoid another apology. "I'm Tallie, your … roommate?"

"Carinne," she said, looking up from her notebook with a closed, but friendly smile. It was less in her mouth, and more in the way her eyes crinkled around the expression. She bent over her notebook and continued writing.

I surveyed our room. Plain concrete floor, textured white paint on the walls and ceiling, and one narrow window looking out over the dumpsters behind the building. A neon graffiti blanket and several black pillows adorned Carinne's bed. Mine, with a large cardboard box sitting on top, had one flat pillow in a white case and a gray blanket. There were two desks in the room: one empty and one stacked with papers, books, and scattered pencils.

Not wanting to interrupt Carinne's train of thought, and needing to be alone with my own, I moved quietly to my bed and opened the box. Clothing was stacked to the top. I grabbed the first few items, desperate to replace the ceremonial outfit, and glanced around. A garment rack hugged the back wall. There were no other doors, meaning no closet and no private bathroom. I would have to brave the hallway to find the bathroom to get dressed.

Vance could still be out there.

Carinne must have sensed my hovering indecision because she spoke without looking up. "You can change in here. I won't look."

With a sigh of relief, I tore the drapes from my shoulders and let them fall in a heap onto the floor. My feet itched to stomp on them, but I finished changing into my leggings and tunic instead.

When I reached my hand back inside the box, a thought struck me.

My parents packed this after the ceremony, without time for sentiment or a note. The hope welled inside me just the same, that they would have included some memento to remind me of their love. Unless their disappointment and shame outshone it all. I was their only child, so all their parental pride rode on me. Maybe I didn't deserve a token of love. The possibility that the box contained nothing personal wouldn't leave my mind. The risk was too big, and my emotions were too raw. I took my hand out of the box, hefted it up in both arms, and deposited it onto the floor. I could pick an outfit from the top every day and deal with whatever was or wasn't in the rest of the box as it came.

Carinne snapped her notebook shut. "I'm grabbing some food. Want me to show you the cafeteria?"

I shook my head. Everything had bunched up too tightly inside me to leave any space for food.

Carinne shrugged and left the room.

Alone, I had nothing to distract me from remembering the ceremony and the odd, whirlwind meeting with *the director*. He mentioned discretion but didn't bother to give me a good cover story, like what craft could possibly be interesting enough to abandon Seerdom for. What would he do, anyway, if I told the truth? Whatever Seer saw me becoming one of them had made a mistake. Their prediction had been wrong.

A shudder ran through me at the thought.

It was impossible. No one questioned the sanctity of predictions from the Oracus. I must have failed or not worked hard enough, forcing my predicted future to change. I wasn't worthy of that future anymore, and no one had considered double-checking the list before the ceremony.

My deficiencies were the best explanation. The thought of admitting that I wasn't good enough after working so hard—it nauseated me to the point of dry heaving. If anyone asked, I would say I had refused Seerdom. From here on out, it was my choice.

I knew, though, that I didn't have a choice at all.

CHAPTER 4

Carinne brought me a muffin and juice from the cafeteria the next morning. I hadn't stayed awake to see her come back from her trip there the day before, so fatigued by grief that I slept for almost twenty hours. My head swam in a groggy sea of incomprehensible dreams, but I was aware enough to thank my roommate for bringing me food.

She shrugged again. "I can't let you die or anything," she said, smiling in her friendly, closed-lip way.

We walked to the basement meeting in companionable silence with about one minute to spare before the orientation took place. We snuck into the back row, finding two of the last seats available.

I didn't want to look, but my eyes ignored my feelings as they scanned the room for Vance. His hair stuck out in any crowd. He sat in an aisle seat, about halfway to the front. With a lurch, I recognized the long, straight black hair on the girl behind him as she leaned forward and rubbed his shoulders. My eyes at least agreed to dart away from that revolting moment.

Next to Vance—no way. Hudson and Mink? They were his best friends back when I knew them all. They were a couple then, inseparable, and it appeared nothing had changed over three years. Butterflies rioted in my stomach. I almost desperately wanted them to take me back as their friend. I had loved them. But Vance's words from yesterday dashed any hope for a joyful reunion with the crew.

Near them, I spotted some familiar faces from the mud incident the day before. It seemed the crew had stayed the same. With one new, notably female member.

Maybe there was only ever one spot available for a girl in their ranks—one who was smitten with Vance. My role was gone, replaced by another, and I'd have to accept that. Not that Vance ever returned my feelings anyway.

A screech rang through the room.

The man on stage grimaced at the microphone he held. "Every year, we start with hearing damage," he said. "Anyway, welcome to orientation for prospective apprentices. I'm going to go over the different trades with openings. Tables along the side wall," he said, gesturing with an apathetic wave, "have a representative from each trade. You can talk to them about their programs. The only requirement is that you start a trade and continue in that trade. That's how you keep your room and board and your living stipend." He listed, rather dully, the different trades. Masonry, electrical, agriculture, sanitary, manufacturing.

With each name, my heart sank lower. I was a kid when I found out I was destined to become a Seer. I hadn't planned for anything else. I didn't know anything else. How was I supposed to choose a trade to work in for *life* if I didn't even know what I could do?

"And new this year," he said, "the Oracus is hosting a competition. Prove yourself in possession of a strong latent Seer talent, and you may be admitted into Seerdom, without having been Foretold."

I gasped and clutched Carinne's arm, making her jump in her seat and stare at me, perplexed.

"Sorry," I whispered.

"It's cool."

This was my chance. If I hadn't deserved it before, I could prove myself in whatever competition they were holding. I could earn my way back into Seerdom. The room faded away as I pictured myself meeting and exceeding all expectations in the competition. My Seer talent wasn't even latent. I had excelled in all my studies. Granted, I had given myself dozens of panic attacks from the stress of staying on top, but I could do it. I had the ability, and it was the only way for life to make sense again.

"For those of you interested in the competition," he continued, "don't ignore the trade tables. Those who lose will accept apprentice positions in whatever trades are still open." He paused to level a serious stare, sweeping it across the room to encompass everyone. "Sign up for the trade you want now. Don't hedge all your bets on this or get excited because they're televising it. None of us knows what the future will bring."

That was his parting line. Not knowing the future. I wanted to cry.

The crowd of at least five hundred people stood from their chairs and made a mass migration to the tables, but the only word I heard repeated over and over was "televised." That meant, in order to watch, people would have to seek out the handful of working televisions in town.

Carinne hung back with me.

"What are you interested in?" I asked.

Carinne shrugged. "None of them. I know I need to pick, but I wish writing was a trade. Poetry owns me, always, but it's so hard to find patrons, I know it's not feasible." She shook her head, her hair falling farther over her eye. "What about you?"

"I'm thinking about the competition," I whispered.

Carinne pushed her hair back to stare at me, unobstructed. "You trust it?"

Her question took me by surprise. "Why wouldn't I?"

"Uhhh," she drew the sound out, giving me time to catch on. "Elites aren't exactly known for elevating others who weren't Foretold. The whole thing feels sketchy."

I shook my head, unable to make sense of her fears. "The nation needs more Seers if they want to stay ahead of things and have eyes on the future of different aspects. Maybe they didn't get enough candidates the regular way."

I shouldn't hint that one Foretold candidate hadn't made it through the gates—the reason for this new competition. They had counted on a certain number of new Seers, and one spot was vacant. The nation already had plans in place for what I would have focused my foresight on in the Oracus, and now that aspect would remain unwatched.

"Come on," Carinne said. "We both need to be realistic."

She walked to the tables, and I trailed after her, listless in my movements. I picked up a brochure at the electrical table, then dropped it right away. Construction-related trades wouldn't suit my unimpressive musculature. I moved to vacate the area, thinking I'd look at culinary next when I ran into a hard, immovable body.

"Oh, I'm sorry," I said before glancing up.

I should have looked before apologizing. Julion, one of Vance's friends, stared down at me with his arms crossed over his chest.

"What the hell do we have here?" he mused; brown eyes narrowed under his dusky blond hair. "What are you doing at the dormitory?"

"Um, I—well, I—" I stammered gracelessly. I had decided on my cover story, but it was difficult to speak under the demanding derision of my former friend. Julion was never one of the guys I got close to.

Julion snorted. "Hey, guys, look what I found. Anyone got a balloon left? I knew we missed a spot yesterday."

Who was he calling over? What if the whole crew ganged up on me? Black dots danced around the edges of my vision, encroaching rapidly as my breathing grew shallow. I could only see what was in front of me, and unfortunately, that was Julion's sneer, not at all softened by his sculpted lips or thin nose.

"I don't know why you're here, Natalie, but me and the boys should plan a welcome back to the neighborhood bash just for you. We'll make it a surprise. Can't wait." He said it all with a straight face, frost in his eyes, then turned to catch up with his crew.

I sucked in quick breaths, pressing a hand against my chest. What kind of surprise? I knew it would be bad, but the options for unpleasant surprises were endless.

"Tallie? You okay?" Carinne came up behind me. "You were supposed to be a Seer?"

I shook my head. I couldn't reply. My throat was full, and my vision wavered. I shut my eyes, steeled myself against the world. When I opened them and found my sight clear, I ran.

CHAPTER 5

Up the stairs to the main level, I flew by Hannah at the front desk, who called out in concern. I ran out of the dormitory building, onto the street, and kept going. There was no destination in mind, only escape. I couldn't face my failure. I couldn't pick a trade. I couldn't face the old friends I'd abandoned. They *hated* me.

Stopping to catch my breath, I leaned against a mailbox. I had to win the competition. I could join Bryla and the rest like I was supposed to. The trouble was, I couldn't recall if the man on the stage told us how to enter.

I had to go back. I would just ignore Julion, Vance, any of the guys. If they tried to taunt me, I would walk away.

"Tallie? Tallie, is that you, honey?"

A screen door slammed shut, and footsteps crunched along a gravel driveway, getting closer.

No. Omen's asshole. Oh, *no*. I recognized that voice.

I had stopped in front of Vance's house.

His mom reached me in the next second and folded me into her arms.

Before I could control myself, I buried my face in her shoulder and cried. She patted my back, smoothed my hair, and murmured sweet things about how I could cry all I needed to.

Vance's mom was the best.

When her shirt was halfway soaked with tears and snot, I sniffled and leaned back.

"I'm sorry for getting you all gross," I said, mustering a weak smile.

"Psh, what's a mother's shoulder for if not the body fluids of her babies? Come in, honey."

She always treated me like one of her own. It helped that she had a dozen kids. One more probably seemed like nothing. By the time I came around with Vance, a lot of his older siblings had grown up and left the house. He was the baby of the family, and his mom was eager to take in an extra.

I relaxed on the way into the house. With Vance at the dormitory, no one else would be there. His dad would be at work, and his siblings would be off living their separate lives with the various trades they had chosen. Vance's mom, Gina, steered me to the kitchen table. She got busy at the stove and soon placed a steaming cup of tea in front of me.

"Which would you like, talking or forgetting?"

Gina's standard question brought me back years to the first time Vance had taken me home with the rest of his crew. My answer hadn't changed in all that time.

"Forgetting, please," I said.

Gina nodded once, then went to the cupboard, moving more stiffly than I remembered. She pulled out a large bowl and set it on the table in front of me. She then moved to the counter and brought more supplies. The same nicked, wooden cutting board she always used, a wide-mouth jar, a rolling pin. Ingredients covered the space next.

I washed my hands at the sink as she finished gathering. When Vance and the other boys ran too wild for my comfort, Gina would steer me into the kitchen with Liann, her second youngest child. The three of us would make pierogi from scratch; huge batches to feed the brood of children Gina and her husband Peter had raised.

"What if I cry into the filling?" I asked, barely audible, even to my own ears.

"Then we'll cut the salt in half and add a little flour to soak it up."

Gina had an answer for everything. For a woman who hadn't chosen a trade—trusting her lifelong sweetheart to fulfill his promises and provide for her—she was remarkably competent. For anyone, she was competent.

She measured and poured the ingredients for the dough, but passed the bowl to me when it was time to mix and knead. Whoever she deemed most in need of distraction got the job of kneading. Mashing the potatoes for filling would be delegated to me today, too. There was no question.

We worked together in a rhythm that hadn't lost familiarity over the gap in years. Gina peppered the silence with tidbits about the neighborhood, her grandchildren, Peter's work. Before I knew it, the pierogi were rolled, filled, folded, and pressed. I slipped them into the large pot of boiling water as Gina heated butter and onions in a separate pan, humming all the while.

A voice called from the rear of the house, "Mom, are there pierogi? Is there cheese?"

I had thought we were alone. Gina, by herself, was safe. No matter what anyone else thought, she made it known I was always welcome in her home. The others, I wasn't so sure about.

"You stay in that bed, Liann. I'll bring them to you when they're done."

"Yes, Mom," came the reply with a beleaguered sigh.

Gina pushed the onions around the buttery pan and spoke in a quieter voice, just to me, "Liann's pregnant." When she looked up, her eyes spoke more of worry than joy. "She's been bleeding off and on with some sharp pains. I had the same with Linus and Greg, but also a few miscarriages in between."

"Has she seen a doctor?" I asked.

Gina pursed her lips and peered into the pot of boiling pierogi. "Not yet, but I know enough to keep her on bed rest. She moved in here for the pregnancy since her husband is too busy with work. Electrical manufacturing." She added a knowing look to her last words that went right over my head.

"I hope everything turns out okay," I said, the words alive in my heart.

Gina had affection, devotion, and wisdom to spare. No matter how many children or grandchildren came into her life, she wouldn't run out. She wanted that baby, fiercely.

After the quiet meal of whipped cheese, onion, and potato wrapped in soft dough, Gina saw me to the door.

"Can you … *not* tell Vance I was here?" I asked, after long consideration. He was her son, which came with some motherly loyalty.

Gina smiled, the well-used lines deepening around her eyes. "If that's what you want, Tallie."

She didn't bother asking if I had seen him or talked to him. For all she knew, I was still on track to become a Seer. That I had come to her for a low-pressure day of being accepted as I was, not who I could be or what I could accomplish. I couldn't shake the feeling that I owed her an explanation—for my choices back then and for now. But she wrapped me into another hug and put a finger over her lips when she stepped back, hushing any words I could have mustered.

CHAPTER 6

Existing in public without my impending Seerdom was like parading around nude. I didn't know who I was or what anyone would see when they looked at me. It could be anything. They could see shame, failure, embarrassment, confusion, heartbreak. Without the shield of being Elite, I didn't know how to put other defenses up. All that warred within me was laid open for anyone's viewing displeasure.

Naked in spirit, I trudged back to the dormitory.

Hannah looked up from behind her desk and eyed me warily.

"Hi," I said, voice meek. "Can you tell me who I need to see to enter the competition? The Oracus one?"

Hannah nodded and shuffled some papers on the desk. They ended up in their original places—a pointless exercise while formulating what she wanted to say. "You're almost ten minutes late to the testing, but I imagine you could sneak in without much trouble," she said. Curiosity glinted in her eyes. "They must be desperate for more Seers."

"Is it in the basement, like before?" I asked.

Hannah shuffled the papers some more, moving the bottom sheet to the top, then back to the bottom. "No, they requested more privacy. They're in the staff room." She pointed a thumb at a door behind her desk. "Go ahead, then."

With a rushed word of thanks, I hurried to the door. I couldn't miss this opportunity. I didn't know how many people would vie for the chance at Seerdom or if any would even possess the latent talent.

About thirty people crowded the small room, some sitting on countertops, and one perched on the lip of the sink. I gawked at the number of them.

Latent predictive powers always seemed like a legend. People talked about them, but I'd never seen any, nor had anyone I knew. A lot of hopes were about to be crushed when all these people found out they were solidly Pedestrian, and my chest ached for them.

I snuck around the back edges of the overheated room, hoping to go unnoticed, until I spotted a familiar auburn head. I stumbled in my gait, pitching sideways into a girl, who lurched into the guy standing in front of her.

"Sorry. Sorry," I whispered, but my wide eyes moved past the disturbance I'd caused to the center of the crowd, where Vance and Em stood. He'd never said anything about wishing to be a Seer. Things change. *People change*, I reminded myself.

"What's this now?" a woman spoke in a clipped tone, the sound of someone overworked and overwhelmed.

"I'm sorry I'm late," I said, cringing as everyone turned to stare at me.

Except for Vance. He glared at the carpet with a determined frown.

"I'd like to enter the competition," I said, my voice rising uncertainly.

The woman, a short but formidable type, sighed with forced volume. "Lucky for you, someone just left us in a most dramatic fashion. You can take his place."

Relief flooded my body, enough to make me wish for a chair to sink into. After passing the test, I'd enter the competition and push myself to win. Then everything would be normal. My parents could come home, and I could rejoin my peers. I wouldn't have to concentrate so hard on looking anywhere but at Vance, because we would never be in the same room together again. I wouldn't feel so lost, cut off from my identity, and cast aside.

Restless anticipation took the place that my worries had vacated. It was only a matter of time.

Something prodded my back roughly, jarring my balance so that I had to lean against a rolling microwave stand. Before I could see who had jostled me, someone pulled the stand from under my hand.

I tipped forward, scrabbling to find something to grab, coming up with only the cord to the microwave.

I fell to the floor and pulled the microwave down after me. It landed next to my head with a jarring crash that left my ears ringing.

"Wow," a male voice sneered. "If you had any Seer talent, maybe you would've seen that coming."

Muffled snickers morphed into outright laughter. I couldn't find the courage to look around to see who had laughed at my expense. I pushed my hands against the ground to stand. Julion was there, upper lip curled in blatant scorn. He was the one who pushed me, then pulled the cart out from under my hand, I was certain.

But what could I say? The woman in charge wasn't likely to investigate, not with her bulging neck vein and rapidly tapping toes. Anything I said would have amounted to stamping my foot and sticking out my tongue, compounding my humiliation. I settled for glaring at his smug face.

Wincing, I crossed the room, putting as many bodies between Julion and me as possible. Throughout it all, I maintained awareness of where Vance stood, so I wouldn't mistakenly look his way.

A girl scoffed and asked, "What's your problem?"

I thought Julion had found a new victim to torment, so I looked for the speaker. It would be easier to stand up for them than for myself. But it was Em speaking to Vance. His eyes remained glued to the floor, shoulders tensed to the edge of breaking, and I didn't know if he had moved once since I entered the room. The only thing I knew was he didn't answer her question.

***

The set-up for testing was awkward and unexpected as if they conceived the process at the last minute. Each individual test was to be performed in private, and the staff room only had one space that met the requirement. The bathroom.

One at a time, Oracus hopefuls entered the bathroom with Adalia, the woman in charge. They stayed for approximately three minutes, then exited, either staying in the room or rushing to leave while not meeting anyone's eyes.

My turn came earlier than I expected.

"Are you sure I shouldn't be last? Since I came in so late?" I asked.

"You're in the time slot of the person who left," Adalia said and beckoned me into the single-stall bathroom.

"I'm so sorry, but is this the official process?"

Adalia scowled at her surroundings. "There are test locations across Michigan. The proctors were instructed to create their own workspaces in the dormitory to which they were assigned. It's about results, not amenities."

I nodded, not wanting to criticize her decision-making. It didn't matter where we were. If I was a Seer, I could see the future in any situation, ideal or less than.

I peered over her shoulder, wondering if entrails were waiting in the sink, but it was empty. I looked for sticks, bones, crystals, cards, any medium that a Seer-in-training could manipulate, but the room was bare, save for the two of us and a toilet.

"Hold still," she said.

Her hands gripped either side of my head and I couldn't move. It was as if my thoughts were sucked out, swirling toward Adalia, totally separate from my brain. My lungs took in air, my heart kept beating. I probably blinked at regular intervals, but until my thoughts were placed back where they came from, nothing else happened inside me.

The room spun as my thoughts returned. I closed my eyes to push back the threatening nausea, counted to ten, then opened again to Adalia's incredulous stare.

"You passed," was all she said, then opened the bathroom door, dismissing me.

In a daze, I rejoined the smaller group of people in the staff room. All eyes trained on me until I chose a spot near the wall and stood still.

I was aware other extra senses existed, but never saw them in action, aside from Seer work. What Adalia had done, stealing and inspecting my thoughts, was unexpected. Frightening.

Adalia ushered through the rest of the people just as quickly until five entrants remained: Julion, Em, Vance, a girl I didn't recognize, and me.

Vance had latent Seer ability. Why wasn't that something I knew about him? Why hadn't he been Foretold in childhood like I had? I hoped I could concentrate on the competition. Vance having a girlfriend, Julion tormenting me—they were distractions I couldn't afford. I didn't know what tasks made up the competition. I didn't know how many other people would be competing from across the nation. I didn't know anything at all.

CHAPTER 7

Carinne paused writing when I got to our room. I hesitated in the doorway; suddenly aware I had left her hanging earlier.

"I'm sorry I ran away," I said.

Carinne placed her pen in the center crease of her notebook and shook her hair aside to look at me. "Stop apologizing."

"Sorry, I'll try." I cringed. "Oops. Not a strong suit of mine." I barely stopped myself from apologizing about apologizing for apologizing.

Carinne smiled with her eyes. "I get it. What happened?"

"I'm not supposed to tell anyone how I ended up here but it's the reason I ran off."

"I'm good with secrets. No pressure, though," Carinne said, shrugging.

"This is kind of a government-level secret. You might not want to know. Or at least, you wouldn't want the government to know you know. They changed my whole life, and my parents', in less than an hour."

Carinne set her notebook aside and scooted to the edge of her bed. "I changed my mind. Now there's pressure. I want to know."

I laughed. For the first time since I'd tried walking through the Oracus gate, genuine laughter spilled out of me. Carinne didn't want to learn a trade, not because she was ashamed of being Pedestrian, but because she longed for something different. She wouldn't be disappointed in me or mock me if she knew.

I locked the door behind me and sat on Carinne's bed next to her, to allow a whispered conversation. "I was one of the Elite."

"Well, I figured you weren't wearing the shoulder drapes for fun. Those are straight-up ugly."

"They feel even worse," I said, trying to cover up my embarrassment that anyone who saw me in those already knew about my failure. "I couldn't enter the Oracus."

"Like, you didn't want to?"

"No, I tried. The wards kept me out. I basically bounced off an invisible shield in the middle of the ceremony."

Carinne waited as I choked down the resurgence of humiliation and heartbreak.

"Everyone else made it through. I was the only one who didn't deserve it."

"Is that how it works, though?" Carinne asked. "I don't think it's about deserving, it's about fate and foretelling."

"But that would mean the Seer who predicted me entering the Oracus was …" I trailed off, unable to speak the blasphemy.

Carinne had no such reservations. "The Seer was wrong."

My breath caught in my throat, and I stared at the door, half expecting the silent men in suits to kick it down and take us to jail.

Director Hooper said I needed to disappear, to never draw attention to myself for the rest of my life. Before dismissing us from the testing room, Adalia reminded us that the contest would be broadcast on the lone network of the nation, reserved solely for government use. Putting myself on a broadcast and seeking the title of Seer would raise questions from those who knew I was Foretold. There was no way the government would allow me to participate—not when crowds of people would gather at the screen sites, eager for a change from the rare directorate-ran news segments.

"Carinne," I gasped. "They won't let me be televised. It would call everything into question."

"So, you're dropping out without even trying?"

Hearing her say it out loud struck me as completely unacceptable. Want and fear took up every space inside me, struggling against each other. "I have to try. But they'll block me from entering, I know it. I'm supposed to lay low, not call attention to myself."

"Could you go as someone else?"

Could I? But there was no one unaccounted for. There was no way to make up an identity, and I didn't know anyone who had one to spare. I had to back out. If I entered as myself, they might not stop at barring me from the competition. The men in suits could come up with a more permanent solution to keep me out of the public eye.

My imagination was running away, but once I thought of it, there it was. It stuck in my mind, growing from a what-if to an inevitability.

"I already gave my name to the woman running the testing," I said. "It's too late to pretend to be anyone different. I have to go talk to her and withdraw."

Hanging my head, I made my way to the main floor. Hannah was behind the desk, as always.

"Hi," I said. "Is the woman from the testing, Adalia, still here?"

Hannah nodded and hooked a thumb back toward the break room.

I let out a relieved sigh. If she had already left to submit my name for the competition, I didn't know what I would have done. Waited for the consequences, I supposed.

Adalia sat at the round table in the middle of the staff room, staring at the top sheet on a short stack of papers. She looked up when I entered.

"Natalie Kowalczyk. Just who I was thinking about." She tilted her head toward the stack of papers.

My name was written across the top sheet. Notes were scrawled underneath, but nothing I could read from a distance.

"I'm here to withdraw from the competition."

Adalia reared her head back, gasping sharply. "You can't!"

"What?"

"Your reading. It isn't latent, Natalie. You have Seer power woven through your neurons. It's a wonder you weren't Foretold. The nation needs you and your talent."

"That's just it. I *was* Foretold."

Time seemed frozen as the words I blurted echoed through my mind. I was reckless, negligent with my own safety. This was the second person I'd told in the last fifteen minutes.

Adalia furrowed her brow and gathered her papers closer to her; an ineffectual shield against what I was going to say.

"At the Oracus entrance ceremony, something went wrong, and I couldn't get in."

"Were you late?" Adalia asked. Conceiving anything other than a Foretold reaching their fate wasn't an option.

I shook my head. "I wasn't. My name was called. I tried walking through the gate, but the wards wouldn't let me through."

Adalia scooted her chair back from the table, eyes darting around like she needed a place to run, but she stayed seated. "That's impossible. You must be lying. Or you had a head injury and can't remember."

I paused, considering her options. Anything was more feasible than a Seer being wrong. But I knew I wasn't lying. There weren't any bumps on my head. I had been there. I knew what had happened.

"It's why I'm withdrawing," I said. "I'm supposed to fade into obscurity in some apprenticeship, not draw attention to myself. Being broadcast won't exactly be following the rules."

"But you have to." Adalia leaned forward, eyes boring into mine with dilated pupils that ate up the surrounding blue. "You must enter the Oracus. It was predicted by a Seer, so it must come to pass. There was a mistake at the ceremony, and this competition is the perfect opportunity to right that wrong. You must enter, and you must win. It's the only way to make it right."

I had thought the same thing, until I realized it would be in direct opposition to Director Hooper's command. "But—but I can't," I stammered. "I'm supposed to disappear."

Adalia drummed her fingers against her thigh, pursing her lips in thought. "What if you entered under a different name?"

Her, too? Maybe she was related to Carinne.

"What different name, though?" I asked. "Why is this so important to you?"

"Maintaining the veracity of the Seers should be important to everyone. The name might be difficult, unless there is someone you know, not in a registered trade, who you trust enough to let you use their identity."

I shook my head. "I agree, but there's no one I can ask."

Adalia's skin paled, and she dropped the papers back onto the table with trembling hands. "If your Seerdom doesn't come to pass, how can we trust any future?"

I searched for an answer but came up short. The words "we can't," persisted in my mind, no matter how viciously I beat them back. In the silence of the room, I heard Vance's name, spoken by a familiar voice outside the door.

"Sorry," I said to Adalia. "Just a minute." I popped my head out of the staff room and saw Gina standing in front of Hannah's desk with a covered dish.

"Vance Oleski," she said. "I wondered if I could drop off some pierogi for him."

"What's pierogi?" Hannah asked, a wrinkle in her voice.

"An edible hug," Gina replied. Her eyes moved past Hannah and lit up when she saw me. "Ah, Tallie! How lovely to see you again."

A fledgling idea prodded at me, but it would be uncomfortable. It would require asking an enormous favor from people I had abandoned for years.

Not asking cost more than I was willing to pay.

"Gina?" I asked, stepping fully out of the staff room. "Can I walk you home?"

"Of course, Tallie," she said, placing the dish on Hannah's desk. "Let's walk."

We stepped into the dusky late evening, arm in arm, and stayed silent until we reached Gina's front door.

"Earlier, you chose to forget but I think you're ready to talk," she said.

I nodded, sudden shyness stealing my voice.

"Is this an indoor conversation?" she asked.

I nodded again and was welcomed into her home for the second time that day.

As soon as the door shut, I started speaking. I told Gina the whole tale, starting with the ceremony and ending at being unable to enter the Oracus Test under my name. I tried my hardest not to focus on the tears shimmering in her eyes. My heartrate sped up, thready and ineffective.

"I'm sorry this is asking so much," I said, looking down. "Too much. But Liann is going to be here, in bed, for months. The competition will take two weeks, at most, they said. So, I was wondering—" I stopped there. It was the biggest imposition I would ever ask of anyone. I'd thought I could do it, but I couldn't. It really was too much. I shook my head. "Sorry, never mind. I should go back."

"Tallie." Gina bracketed her voice with steel; it was her mom tone, honed on the childhoods of her many children. "Ask what you came here to ask."

I squeezed my eyes shut. "Do you think I could ask Liann if I could enter the competition under her name? She's close enough in age, she's not registered for any trade, and she won't be out in public for the next couple of weeks." The words spilled out, tumbling against one another in my haste to get it over with.

I peeked one eye open. I was alone. Opening the other eye, I peered into the hallway connected to the kitchen. I didn't know what to do. Leave, perhaps? Hope Gina didn't complain to Vance that I was harassing his family?

"Tallie, come here, please," she called from the rear of the house.

Heart clogging up my throat, I walked down the hallway to the rear bedroom where Gina perched on the edge of Liann's twin-size bed.

Vance's sister, older by eleven months, had missed out on the red hair. Instead, she was brunette, several shades lighter than my dark hair, with brown eyes. She didn't escape the freckled face that all Vance's siblings sported. There wasn't any evidence of a protruding belly under the sheet that covered her, so I assumed her pregnancy was early on.

"We're all mad at you," she said, by way of greeting.

I nodded, pinching my lips between my teeth.

"Liann," Gina said, her voice low and drawn out in warning.

"Lucky for you," her daughter continued, "I am so bored being stuck in bed, I could die. Watching someone compete to be a Seer using my name could be interesting."

My eyes flew wide open on a gasp. "Really? Truly?" A detail snuck through my elation. "But how can you watch from bed?"

Gina sighed. "George Pappas, Julion's father, has an old wheelchair we can borrow. Watching Vance compete is the *only* time she'll be getting out of bed."

Liann nodded, then her eyes narrowed at me. "Fix your hair. I don't want all of Michigan thinking I don't condition."

I hopped up and down before gaining control of myself. After further discussion and one hundred words of thanks, I rushed back to the dormitory to provide Adalia with my cover identity. Carinne was all too delighted to assist me in lightening my hair and sharing a few cosmetic tricks to sneak past easy recognition. Director Hooper and the silent men in suits wouldn't look for my face among the contestants, so a passing resemblance shouldn't raise any flags. Without my name, I could enter the Oracus Test.

CHAPTER 8

The next morning, I stood in the dormitory's foyer with Vance, Julion, Em, and the other girl whose name I had yet to learn. Vance's stare threatened to hammer me onto the floor. I already felt conspicuous, holding my giant cardboard box, while everyone else toted a bag or a backpack.

Adalia hovered over Hannah's desk, the latter looking not too thrilled to have company. I wondered what she did in her downtime that she wouldn't want stray eyes observing. Certainly nothing as damning as adopting an ex-friend's sister's identity to sneak into a contest to win back a jilted Seer future.

I almost toppled over when the top of my box tipped forward with a sudden lurch. Instead of falling to the floor with it, I let it drop from my hands. It landed on its side with a loud thud that had the others jumping in surprise. The top flaps popped open, and half of my clothes spilled onto the floor.

Julion, both hands stuffed into his pockets, showed no sign of having recently moved. But he had to be the culprit—a subtle one. If everyone had seen him topple my box, they'd be staring at him right now instead of me. I hoped.

Blinking back tears of frustration, I knelt on the floor to set the box right side up. I tried to stuff in a shirt, but someone holding leggings got there first. When I looked up, Vance's blue eyes were so close to mine, I gasped. He shook his head, breaking our gaze. With stiff movements, he gathered pieces of clothing and crammed them one by one into the box.

"Thank you," I whispered, reaching for the rest of my things that he hadn't yet snatched up.

"You make no sense," he muttered, then shot to his feet. He stalked back to Em, who had watched the exchange with a bored expression, twirling her hair around a finger.

Once the top flaps were folded together, I kept the box on the floor, not giving Julion another opportunity to mess with me. Through the window, I watched a van pull up to the front of the building. Adalia ushered us all outside and into the van, one by one.

The drive lasted less than ten minutes. We parked in front of a large brick building that looked more like a mansion than a dormitory. Adalia got out of the van and opened the sliding back door to usher the rest of us out. Our van was one of many parked on the street, with similar scenes playing out next to them. The other contestants.

A middle-aged man waited in front of the door to the building, wearing a button-down shirt and a tie. Next to him stood a woman in plain leggings and a tunic, similar to my preferred style. She held a black device with a large circle protruding from the front. I'd never seen anything like it.

I hovered on the sidewalk, unsure where to go. Looking back toward the van, I watched Adalia get in before it drove away. How precarious had my position in life become that I gasped at the pang in my chest watching her go? I'd spoken to the woman a handful of times, and her loyalty belonged to the needs of the Oracus, not to me. She was also the only person here who knew about my situation and who might have my back.

"Missing someone, Tallie?" Julion asked, walking up beside me with a predatory gleam in his eye.

Panic lanced my chest. What if someone heard my real name and outed me to the competition officials? I pinched my lower lip between my teeth, stopping myself from answering. Sweat beaded on my palms as I stared into the distance, pretending that the name Tallie meant nothing to me.

Julion made a noise halfway between scoffing and laughing. "Figures," he said, then left me behind to gather in front of the building with the other contestants.

There were enough of them to give me a small amount of anonymity, so I waited for Vance and Em to join Julion, then I walked to the other side of the crowd, using the size of the cardboard box to block my face, no matter how my arms protested at holding it higher.

"Hey," a voice at my side said. "I'm Ethyl."

It was the girl from my apprentice dormitory. So much for anonymity. Except, we'd never actually met. I only recognized her face from a few glimpses.

"I'm Liann," I said, hoping she couldn't tell how my heart raced and my stomach lurched at the lie. I held my breath, waiting for her to call my bluff, to shout out my real name, ending this charade before I could even step into the competition building.

She nodded, sending her blonde ponytail swaying, then turned her attention to the man standing before us while rubbing a finger under her nose. Slowly, careful not to let her hear, I released a long, shaky breath that shuddered through my core.

"Welcome to the Oracus Test," the man said, projecting his voice into the cool morning air. "My name is Ridley Marcus, and this is our camera operator. She will record video of each test, as well as the results, so the process can be broadcast to the nation."

The woman held up her black device.

So that was a camera. I wasn't the only one in the crowd bobbing my head around to check it out from different angles.

Ridley clapped his hands and rubbed them together. "We'll start the first test as soon as you get sorted into your rooms and drop off your belongings. No time like the present to secure our futures."

He and I agreed on that point. My future felt anything but secure, and I couldn't wait for that to change.

CHAPTER 9

Intestines were more accurate when I harvested them myself.

With a sigh of resignation, I plunged both hands into the bucket of thawing entrails someone else had procured. The softest bits lodged under my fingernails as I dug deeper, but my mom wouldn't be around to nag about the state of my fingernails after the divination. It took longer than usual, not knowing what type of animal they were from.

Focusing on the assigned question, I pulled two lengths of intestinal tract from the bucket. I relaxed my grip, and they fell to the floor without a hint of a squelch. Frozen innards *technically* worked as a substitute, but nothing rivaled fresh and warm for quality results.

The camera moved into my line of sight. I angled my body so no one watching would have a full view of my face, but I couldn't be sure it was enough. How far did its eye reach? A shiver ran up and down my back as I imagined Director Hooper and his men in suits breaking down the door to arrest me. I had to make this count.

I shoved thoughts of intestinal deficiencies and directorial deceptions aside to concentrate on the curves and intersections sprawled on the floor. After a handful of seconds, the answer appeared in my mind. Twenty-five contestants would pass the first test. A trivial question for divining—something that first-year Foretolds could answer. Contestants could pass with a lucky guess alone. Not me. I scooped the intestines off the floor and deposited them back in the bucket. Swirling them together with the others took an extra minute, but I didn't want someone to pull my answer right off the top of the heap.

I wrote my answer on a slip of paper, folded it, and passed it to Ridley. He opened the paper out of sight of the other contestants, who waited on the other side of the room, and I watched as he wrote it next to my name. Not my real name, though. My assumed identity of Liann Yassin—Yassin being her married last name.

Mindful of the camera, I walked to the sink across the room, scrubbed the intestinal remnants off my hands, and returned to my fellow contestants. Including me, there were fifty. *Fifty* people had passed the assessment for latent Seer talent, and that just included the ones who applied.

I was the twentieth person to take a turn with the intestines. After watching the nineteen before me, I was certain no one else had handled guts before.

Ridley called Em's name. She took long, swaggering strides to the bucket and stuck one hand inside. After a momentary, half-hearted swirl amidst some irregular breathing, she removed her hand and turned to the rest of us, exaggerating a grimace. A few laughs scattered through the crowd of contestants. I didn't hear Vance's among them.

She crossed to the sink and washed her hands, making me realize I had touched the paper and pencil while intestinal matter still covered my hands. Hazards of being used to the medium. After a thorough washing, she bypassed the small table with paper and pencils, moving straight to the man presiding over the test. She stood almost as tall as he did, and she pressed against his side, whispering directly into his ear. Without watching him record her answer, she flounced back to the group with the air of someone who always stood out in a crowd, no matter the size.

No wonder Vance was smitten.

The next contestant was Ethyl. Her shaking hands lowered into the bucket. She didn't take any time feeling around for the proper set of entrails. She merely dunked her hands, then yanked them out, letting multiple lengths of intestines fly where they would.

With a small shriek, she stepped back from the mess she made.

My stomach turned as guilt seeped in. None of them had training in the assisted forms of divination. This was likely their first exposure, while Foretold students practiced every method for years. I had to win, but the unfair advantage festered in my belly.

Ethyl took almost twenty minutes staring at the scattered intestines. What a dull broadcast for the viewers—Liann would be disappointed. Ethyl finally washed her hands, provided her answer, then fled back to the group without picking up after herself.

Judging from her pale skin and glazed eyes, she would faint if she had to touch the entrails one more time. I bolted to pick up the intestines before Ridley insisted that Ethyl do it herself. Before I touched one, the sight gave me pause. The answer was there in how she had scattered her materials.

The entrails hadn't spelled it out, but with the right glance, they gave the impression of the correct number. Was that a coincidence, or did Ethyl truly have latent ability? I hurried to pick them up and deposit them back in the bucket. I washed up and returned to the back of the room, belatedly remembering the camera. *Don't draw attention.*

"Thank you," came a whisper from behind me, where Ethyl stood in my periphery.

I shook my head, denying the need for thanks. *Don't draw attention.*

After the divination, the group was herded out of the room and sent to the upper floors of the giant house we'd call home during the competition. The others fanned out in groups or couples, finding common areas in which to socialize or heading to their assigned bedrooms. I was alone in my quest for the kitchen. Perhaps no one else's stomach had recovered from touching animal guts.

I pawed through the baskets of fresh fruits, dried cherries, and boxed crackers, searching for a snack. I picked up an apple, about to take a bite, but a pointed cough startled me into dropping the fruit.

"Sorry," I said without looking at the cougher.

"What exactly are you apologizing for?"

It was Vance.

"For dropping my apple," I croaked, bending to retrieve it from under the table.

When I straightened, I stumbled back a pace. He stood in the doorway, across the room, but his gaze drove into me with enough force to bowl me over.

"Funny, there are all sorts of things you should apologize for. Being clumsy isn't one of them."

A memory flashed through my mind, playing as if on a movie screen:

"Are those sweets all for Vance?" Hudson teased when he saw me coming up the block with a tray of homemade hard candies.

"Hudson!" I protested, dropping the tray in my shock that he would announce my crush like that.

The candies scattered on the sidewalk and grass. I bent down to pick them up, my face flaming red when I sensed him. Please, please, don't mention what Hudson said.

"Divination by candy? That's new," Vance said, kneeling next to me and picking up candies. He plucked one off the grass and popped it in his mouth. "Did I just eat someone's future?"

I laughed, always relieved when he pretended my tendency to drop objects was divination practice, not chronic butter fingers. The sound pitched higher, and a little unhinged, when I felt the warmth of his breath waft over the side of my throat.

"Have you predicted my future yet, Tallie?" he asked, a whisper in my ear.

No, he wouldn't be cruel or make fun of me. His friends would, but never Vance. Then it occurred to me—at today's test, Ridley called Vance's sister's name when it was my turn at the entrails bucket. There was no way he hadn't noticed.

"Did you see your mom before we left?" I asked.

His eyebrows sunk low and guarded before he shook his head. "No. You shouldn't have either. You should've stayed gone, Tallie."

The way he said my name hadn't changed. Years later, he still let the first syllable hang on his tongue an extra second, making my heart stutter.

"I had to," I said. "It was the only way."

"The only way to do what?"

"I'm not supposed to say."

"Oh, but you can use my sister's name. Does she even know? Why are you being so secretive?"

His voice never rose, but with each question, he advanced on me until I had to tip my face up to look in his eyes. Our breaths met and mingled in the narrow air between us.

He was the one who never showed up that night three years ago.

He was the one who never responded to my letter.

What right did he have to demand anything from me?

He hadn't cared enough about our friendship to let me down easily from my crush. Instead, he left my confession hanging in silence for three years.

"If you wanted to know my secrets, you're three years too late." I side-stepped him and fled from the kitchen, tears stinging my eyes. I only hoped they didn't start falling until I was out of his sight.

* * *

Ethyl hadn't stayed in the common areas to socialize with the others. She was lying in bed, holding a creased, yellowing book three inches from her face. Our other two roommates were gone. She folded the corner of her page down and set the book aside when she saw me come in.

"How could you handle touching them?" she asked, sitting up cross-legged.

"I'm sorry?" I asked, wiping my damp cheeks. My mind was stuck on the interaction with Vance.

"The … guts. You made it look so easy."

Of course, people would ask questions about my experience with the various forms of divination. As a Foretold, I'd trained in assisted divination for years. But if I was supposed to be Liann, I needed to figure out a cover story. I wished I could trust anyone who asked, but it would spread doubt about the Seers. That would not only undermine my future, but like Adalia and Director Hooper said, the structure of our society in Michigan.

"Butchers," I blurted out.

"Huh?" Ethyl asked, wrinkling her nose at me.

"My parents were butchers and they wanted me to learn, too." It was only a partial lie.

My father worked in the culinary trade prior to our family becoming Elite. My parents never encouraged anything but my future as a Seer, though. They had forbidden anything that might get

51

in the way, including friendships with Pedestrians, like Vance and his crew. When they found out where I'd been spending my free time, they flipped and wouldn't let me see the guys again. Afterward, countless hours were spent instructing me to embrace my role as a Seer and as an Elite, and how important it was to serve the nation. They were right, of course, but they never listened when I told them of my anxiety, the stress, and the panic attacks that came from staying at the top, where everyone expected me to be. I hated disappointing them. They only cared about how I performed in my education as a Foretold. So, I worked harder than anyone else to avoid letting them down. They loved me, with conditions. In the end, was that love at all?

CHAPTER 10

The next morning, twenty-five of us waited in the foyer for the testing room to be unlocked. The group included Ethyl, Julion, Em, and Vance. I didn't know how many had gotten through with a lucky guess on the number, and how many had truly divined it.

I turned at the sound of the front door being opened. Two men in dark suits entered the building, scanning our faces until they landed on mine. Without speaking a word—typical—they marched through the others, who parted easily for them, and each grabbed one of my arms. They steered me through the stares of the other contestants and out the door.

A silver car with tinted windows waited at the curb. One man opened the rear door and encouraged me to enter. That encouragement came in the form of a shove.

I spilled face-first into the back seat. The door closed and locked behind me. Cold, firm hands caught my wrists in a punishing grip and kept me from sprawling across the entire row of seats.

I looked up into the assessing stare of Director Hooper.

"You didn't disappear," he said, adding a *tsk* noise with his tongue.

"I—I," I stammered.

"You are a problem," he finished for me. "One I must deal with immediately. But the question remains—how?"

I opened my mouth to give my answer, but he released my wrists to hold a hand up in my face. I stayed silent.

"We could move you, like we did your parents. We could jail you, which tempts me."

Loud voices erupted from outside, then the two suited men entered the front of the car, started the ignition, and sped away from the competition house. They slowed after a minute, and after enough right turns, I got the feeling we were driving in circles.

"We could dispose of you. Quickly, quietly, but that wouldn't solve the entire problem. We need to answer why a Foretold, instead of working in the Oracus with her peers, is vying for that position on a nationwide broadcast." He ran a hand over his jaw and up one cheek before dropping it to his thigh with a sharp slap. "The problem is your existence. It calls into question the veracity of my Seers."

I wiped my slick palms against the fabric of my leggings, but they dampened again, persistently clammy. He seemed far too casual about discussing ending my life. I wondered how often Director Hooper had his "problems" killed to handle this with such insouciance. A quick scan of the backseat upholstery found no old bloodstains. My eyes shifted back to the director, and I found I couldn't swallow comfortably. Would he do it himself, or leave me to the men in suits?

"We will make an announcement. Admit to abandoning your Seerdom then having a crisis of conscience," he said.

I slumped against the car door, on the verge of crying with relief that he wouldn't murder me.

"The story will continue that after such betrayal of your duty to the nation, we required that you prove your devotion through this competition."

I nodded too many times, bobbing my head up and down as quickly as I could. This was perfect. I could regain my position, get my parents back, rejoin the others from my class of Foretolds, and be the person I was supposed to be. Instead of the futureless nothing I had devolved into.

"One requirement," Director Hooper said, plucking lightly at an invisible spot on his pants. "You mustn't slip up. You must win. Easily. Any deficiencies or failures on your part will again cast doubt on the Seers' ability to predict an accurate future. I won't allow that to happen."

It came to me then: Hooper had become the director of our nation after the Seers predicted it. Any doubt cast on the Seers would damage the surety that he was truly meant to be our leader. He could be ousted from his position. There would be protests, uprisings, and violence; similar to how it was before the split. Before the states fully separated into different nations, Michigan had gathered as many Seers as possible to keep a step ahead of the other new nations. If our leadership was based on inaccurate predictions we could face internal unrest, but it would also open the door to political takeover by neighboring nations.

No wonder he thought about having me killed.

"I'll do my best," I vowed. "I'm accomplished in each mode of divination, and I'll win. I won't disappoint you."

My words echoed what I had told my parents countless times since they caught me fraternizing with Pedestrians instead of practicing and studying endlessly. Back then, the consequence of failure was losing the love and esteem of my parents and dropping from my position at the top of the class. Now, if I failed The Oracus Test, the stakes were much, much higher.

The car eased to a stop, and the silent men in suits exited. I still had my weight against the door and pitched sideways when it abruptly swung open. One of the men grabbed me roughly under the arms to stop me from falling onto the sidewalk.

"Don't touch her like that." Vance stood next to us fuming; his hands balled into fists so tight his knuckles were pure white.

What did he care if they manhandled me? I regained my balance and stood straight, fighting the urge to rub the spots on my arms that were sure to bruise. "It's okay," I muttered, not wanting to cause any more of a scene. "I'm fine."

The man released me, and I tried my best to keep my chin up as I walked toward the building. Vance shadowed me; I could feel him there. Just before I reached the door and grasped the handle, his hand flattened against it, stopping me from pulling it open.

"What *was* that?" he asked.

"Good news," I said, hating how my voice shook. "Your family isn't involved anymore because I'll be competing under my own name."

"You know that's not a real answer."

The gust of his breath warmed the back of my neck and I steeled myself against turning around to see how close he stood. Then he released the door. I pulled it open, and we entered an empty foyer, aside from another one of the men in suits.

The man gestured to the testing room in a way that had me hustling, but Vance beat me to the door and held it open for me. What did skipping the beginning of the test to wait outside for me mean? He acted like he didn't care, but he seemed upset. Maybe he wanted to be sure his sister wouldn't draw the ire of the Directorate.

As he walked straight to Em's side, I grew certain. He was worried about Liann's identity and safety, not mine. It was ridiculous to think otherwise; she was his sister and should receive his concern. I was an ex-friend who humiliated herself by confessing unwanted feelings years ago.

Every set of eyes but his bored into me. I owed an apology to every one of them for creating a distraction. Focus was essential when making predictions. If someone in the room failed the test because I had drawn their mind away from their task, it would create another unfair advantage. I had always dropped whatever was on my mind to turn all thoughts toward the future. It was a standard part of training for Foretolds, but no one taught that to the other contestants.

The man who led the test the day before was gone. In his place stood a woman around my mom's age. She was pretty in an aggressive way, as though she faced the mirror every morning and commanded herself into beauty by spite and fury alone. She narrowed her bright eyes at me, then beckoned me forward with an air of impatience.

"Natalie Kowalczyk, please join me." Her voice had a pinched, nasal quality to it that set my nerves on edge; more than they already were.

Keeping my eyes down, I approached the woman and stood next to her.

After it was clear I'd obeyed her direction, she ignored me to speak directly to the single camera in the room. "This young woman's name was inaccurately recorded, thus you heard her called differently yesterday. This is, in fact, Natalie Kowalczyk, a former Foretold."

Scattered whispers spread through the other contestants. I dared to glance up and was immediately caught in the snare of Vance's gaze.

"Miss Kowalczyk, for the third time, will you please address the issue?" The woman's voice pinched further into a higher octave.

The third time? I tore my eyes from Vance and glanced at the woman.

"I'm sorry. Um, yes, I was a Foretold, but I decided against going to the Oracus. It was a mistake, and I would like to fulfill my Foretelling."

The woman raised her eyebrows, unimpressed and waiting for more.

What other words would satisfy Director Hooper? "I made the wrong choice, but they're letting me prove my dedication by competing."

The woman seemed mollified after that and turned her attention away from me.

Assuming that was a dismissal, I started making my way back to the group of contestants.

"Miss Kowalczyk, where are you going?"

I stopped and turned back to her. Menace shone through her toothy smile.

"It's your turn. Please divine the answer to today's question." She pointed to a large mat on the floor, covered with letters. A long string tied to a plain, golden ring lay next to the mat.

I waited for her to ask the question, but she watched me silently, smiling in that same predatory way as if she would relish watching me fail. The others heard the test question before Vance and I made it into the room, and it appeared she wouldn't repeat it for me. It didn't matter that I could excel at any method of divination. Without knowing what to focus on, there was no way to make a prediction.

As my thoughts raced, my chest grew too tight to take in enough air. I tried anyway, just short of gasping. Faintly, a black dot appeared at the side of my vision, quickly followed by another. It wasn't the time for an attack. If ever, I should've had one when the Director's men stole me away, not when faced with an elementary prediction task. I dug my thumbnails into the skin under the nails of my ring fingers, begging the sharp pain to keep me present and calm. I hoped I had time to divine two answers in the time allotted for one.

I stepped over to the mat and knelt to pick up the string, careful not to touch the ring. If any dirt, dust, or even a germ transferred from my skin to the ring, the swing could be imbalanced, partial, and give a faulty reading. There was no way to know how the others had mishandled it, and the possibilities pained me. I held my arm straight out in front of me, letting the ring dangle at the end of the string.

What question will the other contestants be answering today? Reading minds was impossible. I couldn't see the past, but if there were still people left to complete the task, the question they would answer lay in the future, within my reach.

I studied the ring's path, focusing on the question, *what will the next contestants ask*? Each slight pause over a letter in its swinging and swaying hung in my mind until the answer formed. I switched my focus from one question to the next as quickly as possible, so it would appear I was only getting the answer to one question.

The woman might enjoy interrupting me if I took too long.

I urged the ring along in my mind, willing it to take shorter pauses over letters, trusting myself to catch a rushed answer. Once confident I had received the full message, I dropped the ring to the side of the mat and strode to the table with paper and pencils. I took time to make my answer perfectly legible and handed it to the woman. The performative shine faded from her smile.

I stopped myself from apologizing for my nearness as I hovered over her shoulder, ensuring she gave me credit for exactly what I wrote. Two people would be the champions of the competition. Two of us would be allowed to train in the Oracus. My stomach performed an unnatural twist. What if it was Vance and me? We would be together at the Oracus with nothing but the future.

I walked past Vance on my way to the back of the room. "How many winners will there be?" I whispered, wanting him to know the question. It was only fair.

Em snorted from his other side. "I already told him."

Of course she did. She was his girlfriend. If I wasn't an experienced Foretold, I would have spiraled into the despair of imagining Vance and Em elevated to Elite status, together forever in the Oracus. Rather, it was a question of who would win alongside me.

"Took you long enough," Julion mocked. "Didn't they have time for the alphabet in Seer school?" His words rang out over the crowd, inspiring more than a few laughs at my expense.

I spent the rest of the test staring at the ground, thumbnails pressed under my ring fingernails as hard as I dared.

CHAPTER 11

Everyone crowded the kitchen after the test. Suspending a ring over letters didn't put off anybody's appetite. I waited for an opening, grabbed a handful of almonds and an apple, and rushed out of the room.

In the foyer, two vastly different sights stopped me in my tracks. One was a man in a gray suit. He could have been one who took me for a drive earlier that day, but with their shaved heads, pale skin, and identical outfits, they all looked kind of the same. When it didn't appear he would approach me, I allowed myself to pay attention to the other person in the room.

"Carinne!" I gasped. "What are you doing here?"

My roommate of two whole nights at the apprentice dormitory stood carelessly close to the suited man, holding a notebook by her side. She shrugged and crossed the room to stand in front of me.

"There's no rule against visiting contestants. It's not like any Seers are going to show up here and give away the secrets of prediction. Just Pedestrians with our general uselessness."

"I'm happy to see you," I said quietly, hoping she heard my sincerity. I lost every one of my school friends during the Oracus entrance ceremony. Not that we'd been close. The best friends I'd ever had were lost years before.

"I made you something." Carinne opened her notebook and tore out a sheet of paper, leaving the edges ragged.

I started reading as soon as she handed it over:

Being a spy isn't her trade. She snuck in but already got made. Lucky her future spells S-E-E-R. She belongs in the Oracus, where she'll go far. I'll be cheering from the galley. Good futures to you always, Tallie.

Next to the poem was a sketch of me, my face shockingly accurate, in the traditional garb of a Seer, with a shining glow surrounding me. I clasped the paper to my chest and laughed, filling with a lightness that mirrored the picture.

Carinne smiled, showing her teeth for the first time in front of me. Her entire face changed in a show of radiance. "And this is why I create. Making people feel like that."

I wiped away a sudden, embarrassing, out-of-place tear and leaned forward to grab her in a hug. The paper crinkled in protest between us, and I jumped back to smooth it out.

"I better go," she said. "Tomorrow's the deadline for picking a trade if I want to have a choice."

"Carinne?" I called out to her before she reached the door. "Don't let anyone choose your future for you."

With a sigh and a nod that looked nothing like an agreement, she headed into the afternoon sun. The door didn't close behind her, because someone held it, waiting to enter the building. I meant to return to my room and find somewhere safe to put the poem and sketch, but my heart froze in my chest.

Hudson and Mink, two of Vance's best friends, entered the foyer. They stopped short when they spotted me.

"Tallie!" Mink said, surprise clear in his voice and his face.

"Or should we say Liann?" Hudson asked, smirking until Mink elbowed his stomach. Hudson caught Mink's arm and wrapped it around his waist, pinning them to each other's sides.

They'd always been cute. Time hadn't changed that. Even if we weren't friends anymore, I would always root for their relationship. I didn't need a Seerdom to see they would make it together. Anyone could tell.

"Sorry," I said. "I didn't have much choice." No good ones, anyway.

Hudson raised his eyebrows. "Still apologizing for literally everything?"

I grimaced and nodded.

"Did you want to say sorry for that just now?" he asked, a grin splitting his face. His ever-present smile was familiar and jarring all at once.

I nodded again, pressing my lips together to hide my answering smile. The crew didn't include me anymore. It might break my heart if I tried to be friendly and got rejected.

"You know, we never thought you abandoned us on purpose," Mink said, inching himself and Hudson closer to speak quietly. "We kind of got the impression your parents wouldn't have approved."

My eyes shot wide open. He pegged it, exactly. "I thought about you, all of you, every day."

Mink put a hand on my forearm. "You were always our favorite girl."

The unwanted, inappropriate tear that threatened to show itself after Carinne's gift returned. I wasn't able to hold it back again, so it slid down my cheek and brought a few friends along with it. I sniffed and brushed my sleeve under my eyes.

"What are you doing?" Vance's voice called across the foyer from the bottom step of the staircase.

I meant to answer, but when I turned around, I saw he had pointed the question at his friends. Mink didn't move his hand right away, instead giving my arm a small squeeze.

"Still our favorite," Mink whispered.

Hudson winked at me, and called to Vance, "You should know already, future boy!"

"It doesn't work like—"

"Eh, you've always been a slow learner," Hudson said. "Remember that jump we built in the woods? Took you a *week* to land it."

"It was more like five days." Mink tried to inject his brand of fairness.

"You mean the one you busted your nose on?" Vance asked with a grin. "You're lucky Mink isn't in it for the looks."

As they laughed their way to Vance, my heart warred between shrinking and swelling.

They didn't hate me. Why couldn't Vance feel the same way? Yes, I had stopped hanging around them in favor of dedicating myself to the life of an Elite, but I had written him a letter to explain, asking him to meet me the next night. I wrote about my feelings that had been brewing for years, that I would find a way around my parents' rules to keep seeing him. I was specific about the time and place. He was the one who never showed up.

Once the boys vacated the foyer to hang out somewhere else, I found myself alone with the director's suited man. He crossed the room in a few long strides.

"Careful with your visitors," he said, not as silent as I had expected. "Don't let anything slip. Or the Director might ask that I slip."

The man patted a pocket in his suit jacket, and I didn't want to guess or divine what was inside. Clutching my gift from Carinne, I fled up the stairs to my room.

Ethyl was inside, reading again. This time, she didn't put her book down, but spoke to me from behind the pages. "You were Foretold," she accused in a dry tone.

"I'm sorry. It was supposed to be a secret." I hovered by the door, not sure she'd welcome me in after finding out I'd lied.

"The butcher story didn't pass the smell test," she said.

"The smell test?"

"Whenever someone lies to me, I get a whiff of burnt rubber. I hate when people lie, mostly because it smells disgusting." She shuddered slightly.

"You have extrasensory talent," I said, inching a little further into the room. "I never knew so many people had it, outside of … you know."

"Foretolds? Just because we didn't luck out with strong predictions doesn't mean we aren't as useful as people like *you*." She practically spit out the word, knuckles whitening as she gripped her book. "Not that we'll get a fair shot. You've trained in all of this, so obviously you're going to win. That leaves space for one other winner. I'm done for."

I gaped at her. "That means you know there will be two winners. Have you ever done this type of prediction before? With the weighted ring?"

Ethyl shook her head.

My mouth hung open farther. How had she been missed in all the rounds of Foretelling?

"That's amazing," I said. "You *should* be in the Oracus. You should have been Foretold with natural talent like that."

"It doesn't matter," she muttered into the book's pages, as it slowly moved to cover more of her face. "None of us have a chance with you around."

That weight of shame and guilt over an unfair advantage sloshed in my belly and I wanted it gone. "I'm sorry. I really am. This is completely unfair."

Ethyl shrugged. "That's nice, but those are just words. They don't change anything."

She was right. Director Hooper would hate it, but … "What if I taught you?"

Ethyl dropped her book to her chest, revealing wide eyes and an open mouth. "You would do that?"

"Yes!" I exclaimed without hesitation. "But would it be okay if I offered it to everyone else, too? I wouldn't feel right only helping one person."

Ethyl sat up and scooted to the very edge of her mattress. "You'd still have a leg up, but at least we'd have a chance. You won't trick anyone, right? Like, no false information or holding things back?"

I shook my head enough to make myself dizzy. "I promise."

Ethyl stood and held out her hand. I grabbed it and we shook, with all the formality of a treaty between nations.

"You can't learn everything in one day," I said. "We'll need to know what the test is about tomorrow and focus on that."

I looked around for some type of divination material. The standard methods involved entrails, ring and letters, bones, sticks, flame, melted wax, arrow shafts, lightning, midnight ring singing, and avian behavior. Our room was devoid of all those things.

"Will you spread the word?" I asked. "Ask the others to meet in the living room for a lesson? I need to find supplies."

Ethyl bolted from the room.

I had no idea non-Elites would be so eager for a shot to get into the Oracus. It shamed me that I hadn't considered it. Elites had access to better lifestyles, better healthcare, more money, and all the privileges of elevated status. I'd heard that trade and commerce were huge before the states split apart. People had access to almost endless supplies of anything they wanted. It was unimaginable, though I'd never been without anything material after being Foretold. It was no secret the nation's finite supplies went to Elites first.

Making up my mind, I left the room, hustled down the stairs, and walked outside to gather sticks of similar length and girth. Preferably all from the same tree, for the highest accuracy. Sticks tended toward irregularity, but they were the most readily available material.

Weather-wise, it had been a calm spring. There were too few fallen branches available on the ground. All the smaller ones I could snap off by hand were up high. One gnarled oak with a split trunk grew in the front yard of the dormitory. I stuck my foot in the V created by the split and hoisted myself up to stand in it. There was a branch thick enough to support my weight, but it was farther up the trunk than I could reach.

I glanced ruefully at my leggings, saying goodbye to the intact fabric over the knees. I wrapped my arms around the trunk and worked at shimmying my way up the slant of the tree. Red-faced and straining, I reached my target branch. This was the tricky part. I hadn't climbed a tree since I was a kid, but determination had to count for something. I reached around to the branch, hooked a leg over it, and grabbed hold. When I tried to swing my body around, I tipped to the side.

Shrieking, I held on, but upside down. My arms and legs clung to the branch as I realized there was no way out of this without falling and breaking a bone. I'd already stressed my muscles shimmying up the trunk; they'd never agree to pull my full body weight from this position.

"Tallie? What are you doing?"

I'd recognize his voice anywhere. Even more familiar was the way my name sounded cradled in Vance's mouth.

"Sorry," I called down, unable to look at him. "I didn't really mean to end up this way."

"What way? About to fall and bust your *dupa*?" His voice came from directly underneath me.

If I hadn't needed to concentrate on not falling and busting my butt, I would have laughed at his terminology. To Vance's grandparents' chagrin, he'd never picked up any Polish, aside from the swear words.

"Hey, Vance," Mink called from farther away. "Maybe you'd be better off just trying to catch her from down here."

"Not a chance," Vance replied, his voice getting higher and closer all the time. "If she tries hanging onto something, it always ends up on the ground. That probably includes herself."

"*Herself* is right here, guys," I muttered, trying to ignore the growing feeling that my fingers might be slipping. I held on extra hard with one arm while I loosened the other to scoot it farther up on the branch. Repeating the action with the other arm, I laced my fingers together over the top of the branch. I was a little more secure, but I didn't have an exit strategy.

"Tallie," Vance said, "can you shimmy toward me?"

"Where are you?"

A short laugh came from the direction my butt was pointing.

"I'm on the trunk, where it meets your branch."

He had climbed up after me. My heart picked up its pace and sweat slicked my palms. That wasn't too convenient since I was counting on them to stay on the branch.

"Forget shimmying, I'll come to you."

"What if it can't hold us both?" I couldn't hide the shrill fear that laced my voice.

"Sure would be useful if someone could predict that future," he muttered.

The branch shook between my thighs and my arms as it bore his weight. I squeezed my eyes shut and waited, fearing a splintering crack that would herald our imminent fall to the ground. Instead, I felt his nearness and heard his soft whisper next to my head.

"Open your eyes," he said.

"Is he rescuing her or trying to—oof!" Hudson's voice cut off with a grunt, and I could hear Mink shushing him.

I parted my eyelids a centimeter or two. Vance's face hung over the side of the branch, barely above mine. His deep-set blue eyes held the playful spark I used to see so often.

"Hi," I said, my voice matching his whisper.

"Hi," he replied, his gaze holding mine. "Tallie, I have some bad news."

"What?" I breathed out.

"I didn't really think this through."

A choked laugh forced its way from my throat. "That makes two of us."

He continued staring at me, a small smile playing over his lips. They were so close, much closer than I'd ever been to them back when we hung out every day. I'd dreamed of having them this close to me, and closer still.

"I think I've got it," he said, breaking the spell. "When I grab one of your arms, you need to let go with the other. Then reach it around to the side I'm holding you on. We'll hoist you right side up together."

"You won't leave me hanging?" I asked, meaning literally in the moment. My mind raced to the figurative—when he'd left me hanging after my love letter until weeks later, broken-hearted, I'd accepted that he never felt the same.

"I've got you," he said, all playfulness gone from his face.

It would have to do, because the middle of the branch creaked, loud and unsettling. His hands gripped my right wrist, the muscles in his arms straining and tensed. I wouldn't complain, but I'd likely sport a bruise where he held me. I took a deep breath and let go with my left arm. It dangled in the air for a brief, weightless moment, then I snaked it between my chest and the bottom of the branch and reached up for Vance. One of his hands released my right wrist to grab my left. He had me. Just like he said. He had both of my arms securely in his grasp.

"Up you go," he said, voice rough with exertion.

He tugged at my arms, and I shifted my hips upwards, urging any strength left in my torso to haul my weight upwards. With a final burst of strength, Vance pulled me up to the top of the branch, falling back on his butt where it met the trunk. Our momentum pulled me with him, so I ended up tucked into his lap.

The branch, right where my arms had been a second ago, cracked and split, half of it crashing to the ground.

CHAPTER 12

Cringing, I stared down at the splintered branch below us.

Hudson approached it, hands on his hips, and looked up at us. "That would've busted both your *dupas*," he said, voice casual and one eyebrow lifted.

I felt a rumble behind me. Vance was laughing. The sound, deep and rolling and familiar, sent my heart soaring higher than the top of the tree we occupied.

It didn't last long enough.

He steadied me while I situated myself on the trunk, but somewhere in my clumsy maneuvering, his face closed off again. The warmth of the moment was over, apparently. Or maybe I had imagined the whole vibe.

Once on solid ground, he crossed his arms and ran his tongue over his teeth behind his closed lips. "You asked if I would leave you hanging. I'm not you, Tallie." He turned and strode off.

"How is that fair?" I whispered to his back. Building on the adrenaline that hadn't left me, I repeated the words louder, more demanding.

Hudson fake coughed in the wake of my question. "Should we really stand out here talking in this kind of weather?" he asked.

"What?" I looked up at the blue sky, dotted with scattered clouds. What did he—

Hudson, hands stuffed in his pockets, high-tailed it after Vance, whistling a light tune. Mink grimaced, tossed me an apologetic shrug, and followed the others.

I hadn't felt so confused since the moment the Oracus gate rejected me. If pressed, I wouldn't be able to say which moment made me feel lower. But I couldn't wallow in the aftermath of hope, always followed too closely by discouragement. I had to keep my word to Ethyl.

At least one good thing came out of the tree incident. The branch that came down had perfectly sized off-shoots that broke free when it hit the ground. I gathered as many as I could into my sore arms and hefted them back inside the dormitory.

The man in the suit stared at me, expressionless, when I entered. His gaze dropped to my bundle of sticks and stayed there until I walked past him to look for Ethyl.

I found her in the house's sizable living room that hosted three couches, an oversized armchair, two fraying ottomans, and a handful of mismatched dining chairs. Red bricks took up most of the long wall next to the doorway I stood in, surrounding a fireplace. Diamond-patterned carpet covered the floor and faded velvet curtains blocked half of the sunlight coming from two tall windows opposite the fireplace.

Ethyl wasn't alone. Almost every contestant, minus Vance and Em, was present.

I smiled tightly, shy with everyone's attention diverted to my sticks and me. I wasn't sure which direction to look. Someone coughed. The person on the floor next to them looked away, fidgeting with their shoelaces. It was time to say something or scrap the whole idea.

"Hi guys. I'm Tallie. But you probably know that because they announce our names all the time." I took a steadying breath and reminded myself to focus. "Did Ethyl tell you what's going on?"

"I did," Ethyl spoke up from her spot on one of the dining chairs. "What's with the sticks? Our first lesson?"

Next to her sat another one of our roommates, Kinsley. Other contestants crammed four at a time on the couches, sat cross-legged on ottomans, and sprawled on the floor, leaning their backs against legs and furniture.

"Kind of," I said. "I'm going to use them to figure out what kind of test we'll have tomorrow, but I thought I could do that in front of you guys, so you can learn this method, too." I sat in the middle of the floor, cross-legged, and set the sticks down in a pile in front of me. "This is the least reliable form of assisted divination," I said.

"What do you mean, *assisted* divination?" a guy with short, curly hair asked. Maddoc, if I remembered correctly from his turn at the entrails.

"It's what the Foretold learn, using materials other than just our brains. We don't get full access to pure divination until we enter the Oracus."

"So, why'd you bail if it would stick you with—ahem—sticks?"

Ugh, I knew that scornful voice. Julion. He sat in the middle of a couch, two girls on one side of him and a third girl on the other. He had his arms across the back of the couch, and two of the girls were trying to get his hands to drop onto their shoulders. It was difficult not to gag, but drawing his ire would be worse.

"Like I said, it was a mistake." *Please drop it,* I silently begged.

"Mm, I don't buy it," he said with a shake of his head, flipping his light hair away from where it skimmed his eyebrows.

"Hey, do you want to learn this stuff or not?" Ethyl asked, standing up from her chair. Her glasses magnified her glare, and she looked ready to go to bat for me.

Maybe not for *me*. She was probably still mad that I lied to her. She wanted this information, that was all, and Julion was keeping her from learning.

Julion rolled his eyes, drawing out the movement in an obnoxious, performative way. One of the girls under his arm giggled and jabbed his side. He flinched away from the unexpected touch but composed himself quickly.

Had anyone else seen that?

I cleared my throat. "Sorry," I said to the group, blaming myself for Julion's distraction. His suspicions were valid. I scrounged through my broken train of thought. "Um, out of all the methods of assisted divination, this is the one that's easiest to get materials for."

They didn't need to know how I almost fell out of a tree. It hadn't been that easy.

"Before starting, make sure the sticks are all as close in size as possible, and snap off any bits that branch from the sides." As I spoke, my hands moved automatically, snapping side twigs and tearing away too-long tips. In a short time, a pile of nearly perfect sticks lay before me. I gathered them into my arms and stood.

"It's important to push everything else from your mind and only think of the future you seek while arranging your materials. Let that feeling inside you guide your arms when you drop them." I stopped talking to follow my own advice. *Tomorrow's test,* I thought over and over as my arms extended.

In a sweeping arc, I scattered the sticks on the floor.

"That's the part that's most important to concentrate on. You need it while reading the lay of the sticks, too, but not as much as when you let loose of the material."

I walked a tight perimeter around the fallen sticks, nerves and shyness fading away as I found my stride. This skill set was what I had dedicated years to, what my identity, my self-worth, and everything were anchored to.

"They won't spell out letters or take the shape of numbers," I said. "Half of divination is the feeling you get from the arrangement of the material, the essence it provides you, then interpreting that feeling into a solid answer."

Julion snorted. I didn't look, but it had to be him.

"It's hard to teach. It's mostly about practice, then waiting to see if the future you saw came true, then learning from that which feelings to follow, and which to dismiss. I'm sorry you don't have the time for that level of learning." I stopped my pacing and looked around, pausing at a few of the more engaged faces. "I'll try my best to tell you which pieces speak to me most, and the impressions they give me."

"Thank you, Tallie," Ethyl said, a bit too loudly. She had a glare trained on Julion.

"You're welcome," I said. "You don't need to thank me, though. I'm mostly sorry I didn't think to do this before the first two tests."

A creak in a floorboard drew my gaze to the door. Vance, arms crossed, and Em stood just inside the doorway, not fully committing to entering the space and joining the lesson. The underside of my ring fingernails had seen enough action lately. I pressed my thumbnails under the nails of my pinky fingers, forcing myself back to the moment of the lesson, back to the prediction at hand.

"Do you see the way these sticks have formed almost a hexagon? It makes me think of a container. The parallel pieces over here," I said, gesturing, "could represent water. But this grouping here, do you see how most of them have small, swirling knots in their bark? I think that our test tomorrow is going to be hot wax."

I looked up at many pairs of eyes holding blank expressions. "Like I said, it's hard to learn without practice and the benefit of trial and error. Sorry," I added quickly.

"How's that going to help any of us for tomorrow?" Julion asked. "All this does is give you a chance to show off. You think you're better than us. We get it. You don't need to rub it in anymore."

He removed his arms from the back of the couch, stood, and stalked toward the door, where Vance snagged his sleeve. I couldn't hear what he said, but Julion's reply rang out.

"Someone had to say it. I know you never did."

He left the room. Silence descended over the rest of us. I couldn't bring myself to look at Vance.

Thankfully, Ethyl interjected again. "So, what are the tips for hot wax?" she asked. "What do we do with it?"

Needing to stay busy, remembering Gina's lesson to move through feelings, I bent to pick up the scattered sticks from the floor. Talking to a crowd was easier without looking at anyone, especially after being humiliated. Public embarrassment was turning into a habit. Someday I'd find a way to break it—blend into the background and disappear, like Director Hooper had first commanded.

"This kind of prediction requires a bowl of cold water, a metal ladle, a flame, and wax. You heat the wax in the ladle over a flame, then drizzle it into the water. Concentrate on the future you seek when drizzling the wax, then interpret the shapes and patterns of the wax as it lands. But the wax can be finicky. If it heats too much, it'll take too long to cool in the water. Instead of shapes, you'll get a lump that won't tell you a thing."

The guy who had asked about assisted divination, Maddoc, spoke up again, "I don't think I felt any message or essence when we did the intestine test. I stared at them for a while and kept going between twenty-five and twenty-four. Obviously, I decided on twenty-five, but I didn't notice anything about the way it happened that I could repeat. Is this going to be the same?"

I nodded, relieved at the interaction. It meant someone was listening, trying to learn, and that I wasn't just making a fool of myself. The other contestants would only warm up to me if I brought something of value to the table. Just me, myself, my existence; it wasn't enough to earn acceptance.

"The reason you kept seeing those two numbers is because it wasn't certain if you would stay or be eliminated. It was all based on whether you could perform that reading, so the answer wasn't sure until you were."

His face scrunched up in wrinkles of confusion. "But wouldn't that have messed up the reading for everyone before me who wrote down twenty-five?"

I sighed, regretting my own lack of expertise. I hated coming up short. "A lot of Seerdom is not easily explained. People who need rigid, set explanations for things tend to not be Seers. I *wish* I had a better answer for you. I'm sorry I don't know enough."

"Dude." He laughed. "You know so much more than any of us. Don't sweat it. It's not like anyone expects you to be a professional Seer."

I *should* have been a professional Seer already. He didn't mean it in a judgmental way—I didn't think so anyway—but it stung. It put a voice to my own fresh failures.

A few murmurs of agreement sounded throughout the room. Not many, but a few. I looked around for someone who maybe didn't despise me and noticed that Em had fully entered the room, claiming Julion's former spot on the couch, and Vance had left. Disappointment lanced my chest, but I dug in my thumbnails and fought to ignore it.

"I can tell you a couple more tips for this kind of divination, if you want?" My voice trailed up at the end; not sure anyone would take the offer.

"Yes!" Ethyl burst out, and the people sitting closest to her laughed at her enthusiasm. Her entire face flushed, but she didn't back down from it. "Anything can help," she added.

"Okay, well, this might sound weird, but don't look *too* hard when you're reading your material. Note the first area that catches your eye. Most times, that will provide the biggest clue to the future you're predicting." I searched my memory for more beginners' tips. Things that were natural now but required concentration when I was first learning good habits. "Don't phrase your question for the future with tons of words. Keep it as short as possible. If it seems too vague, nudge it along by thinking one, or maybe two clarifying words. Getting bogged down in big, long sentences will distract you from concentrating on what you want to divine. Keep it short. Repeat it like a mantra if it helps you focus."

A girl who had been sitting with Julion stood up, sighing. "I guess we'll see tomorrow if any of this is even true," she said.

The other girls on that couch, aside from Em, rose and followed her out of the room.

"I guess we will," I mumbled in their wake. Turning to the remaining contestants, I offered a weak smile. "If I think of anything else before tomorrow, I'll try to make it to everyone's rooms to let you know. If you want."

Ethyl surprised me by clapping. Kinsley joined in almost immediately, then the others added a few claps of their own. Nothing boisterous or long-lasting, but the scattered applause helped punctuate the end of the impromptu lesson. When I left the room, a suited man was retreating down the hallway toward the foyer. Had he watched the lesson? Maybe he was curious whether I was worth Director Hooper's fuss or not.

The rest of the evening passed slowly, so I went to bed early, trying to hasten time. I wasn't worried about passing the next day's test. Reading hot wax couldn't be simpler. I fell asleep with an unfamiliar feeling of satisfaction from trying to help the others.

CHAPTER 13

I woke with a start in the pitch-black room. Ethyl's quiet snores were steady, and Kinsley's nostril made that faint popping noise it did while she slept. I couldn't tell what had woken me. The air had a new tinge, maybe an extra darkness that spread too far. The slight odor of sweat.

A large hand clamped over my mouth. The sharp prickle of beard stubble brushed against my ear.

"Shut up and stay quiet, or I'll knock you out," my assailant whispered, just over the edge of audible speech.

I did my best to nod, but the hand over my mouth immobilized my head against my pillow. The man lifted me out of bed and hefted me over his shoulder. I tried reaching back to tug down the hem of my oversized sleep shirt. He didn't allow me the freedom of movement.

The man hustled down the stairs, jarring my chin against his back with each step. He held me in place with one thick arm to open the door, then carried me into the cool night. Craning my neck, I saw a silver car that was becoming too familiar, and goosebumps erupted over my bare legs.

Once deposited in the backseat, I wasted no time in straightening my clothing, pulling the long shirt down to cover my thighs. Only then did I meet Director Hooper's eyes. This was un*called* for.

"Don't you have other things to do than kidnap me? Like running Michigan?" The words were out before I gave them permission. I covered my mouth with both hands. "Sorry," I whispered between my fingers.

"Nothing is more important than preserving the reputation of those who staff the Oracus," he said, unbothered by my outburst. "If you simply follow my instructions, these 'kidnappings' won't be required. Nor will the presence of my agents to monitor you."

I knew the suited man in the lobby was one of the director's. I'd thought he was there for general contestant security, though, not to spy on me. At least I knew the correct way to refer to them now. Agents.

"Didn't I tell you to win the competition?" he asked, studying his fingernails on one hand, a picture of detached calm.

I nodded, sensing a trap, but unable to see the trigger that would set it off.

His hand shot out and grabbed the front of my nightshirt, yanking me close to him. My heart stopped, then doubled up on speed to make up for the deficiency. I fought against invisible weights to take a deep enough breath.

"Why are you helping the other contestants? This is stark defiance."

He loosened his grip from my shirt, then shoved me to the other side of the car hard enough that my head struck the window. Wincing in pain, I huddled in the farthest corner of the seat.

"It—it didn't seem fair," I said in a whisper.

"Fair?" Director Hooper laughed, a sharp barking sound, with no enjoyment in his eyes. "You absolute *child.* This concerns the stability of the nation. My authority. Your *life.* What don't you understand? Do you require further incentive to crush your competition?" He paused, closed his eyes, and indulged in a deep sigh. "Make it clear there was a reason you were Foretold. Create no suspicion. Solidify the veracity of our Seers because I'm done with playtime. If you do anything but dominate the other competitors, I will begin removing things from your life that you might not want to live without."

My throat was too dry to swallow comfortably. Tears stung my eyes, and my breaths came too fast. I didn't know what he would remove, but my mind flashed to my parents, wherever they were. Surely, he didn't mean them. Maybe he would just amputate a finger or two of mine; that would be preferable.

"No more failures, Natalie." He rapped his knuckles against the window.

The agent who had remained outside opened my door. On shaking legs, I exited the car and leaned an arm against the frame, trying to steady myself. Pointless effort. Carinne had warned me that the Oracus Test felt sketchy. Maybe she had the reason wrong, that Elites wouldn't elevate Pedestrians, but I shouldn't have dismissed her suspicions.

I staggered back to the dormitory, shadowed by the agent the entire way. Once inside, I staggered toward the wall and slumped against it to catch my breath.

Going to bed was the wisest choice, but I would never fall asleep after being threatened. Keeping one hand on the wall, I made my way to the kitchen. Light spilled from the open refrigerator.

I stopped walking, not wanting to talk to anyone, to pretend things were okay. It was too late for avoidance, though. The person with their head in the refrigerator straightened and glanced around the door.

Julion.

I closed my eyes and stifled a groan.

He stepped away from the refrigerator, not bothering to close the door. I could see half of the cruel smile on his face, only one side illuminated. He took his time looking me over, head to toe, in a way that made my stomach roil in protest.

"I didn't take you for the type to sneak out for some midnight action," he drawled.

I glanced down at my rumpled sleep shirt, noticing too late that the collar had ripped under the force of the Director's grip. The hem hiked crookedly up one thigh. Grimacing, I raised a hand to feel the back of my head. My hair was matted and sticking up from cowering against the corner of the car. There wasn't a way I could defend myself from his assumption, not without spilling the secret of Director Hooper's threats. I was all too aware of the agent in the building.

Julion's stare shifted to a point over my shoulder. I turned to see the agent lurking in the doorway, then caught Julion looking between us. The growing incredulity on his face revealed who he thought I met for that "midnight action."

"Why do you hate me so much?" I asked.

Julion dropped the smirk and looked down his nose at me. "Hate implies strong feeling. I just don't like you. I don't respect you. You rubbed it in all our faces that we weren't good enough to hang around. That was annoying. But the way you messed with Vance, that's what pissed me off."

His words bounced around the confines of my mind, not lining up with each other. I understood why it seemed like I had abandoned them and treated them like they were inferior. I supposed I had, even if it wasn't my idea and I hated doing it. But messing with Vance? The only thing I could think of was that my confession of love disgusted him because he didn't feel the same way and never had.

Unfortunately, being in his presence reminded me that no matter how much my brain understood his rejection, my heart had never forgotten the way he made it feel. Being a part of his circle had brought with it boundless excitement, no matter what mundane day was occurring. At the same time, a sense of security had calmed my deep-seated anxieties. Around him, the pressure of my position dissolved to nothing, allowing me to be free. For the first time since I had been foretold, Vance had helped me feel like *me* and not just a future Seer.

But he was gone from my life, aside from a few uncomfortable encounters. My Seerdom had vanished as well. There was no 'me' left. It felt like I was nothing at all.

I turned and ran from the kitchen, molding my body to the side of the doorframe as I went, trying my hardest not to touch the agent. I wouldn't bolster Julion's assumption.

Safe in my room, with only Ethyl's sleeping form for company, I was free to consider what happened with Director Hooper. I didn't doubt that he would follow through on his threats, but I wanted to be a Seer. His goal and my goal were aligned, at least temporarily. Nothing I had taught the other contestants would give them an edge over my years of practice—not with one short lesson.

There was also the knowledge that a Foretold held more Seer talent than someone with hidden abilities. I cringed at the thought, true though it was. Julion's words echoed in my memory, that I made their crew feel not good enough. It wasn't my fault that the nation needed Seers so much that they were elevated to Elite status. Not *everyone* could be a Seer.

While I acknowledged the bare facts, guilt seeped in through the cracks. I didn't want anyone to feel inferior. I was desperate enough to avoid that feeling myself to ever wish it on another. But Seerdom was all I had; all I was. The other contestants didn't have that pressure riding on them. How could I face them, though, after promising to share my knowledge? I couldn't imagine breaking my word. But teaching them anything else risked the director's retribution.

The others would see me how Vance and his crew had for the past few years. A snobby Foretold, treating Pedestrians as disposable, lesser-than. I gritted my teeth, fighting back tears. A houseful of teens didn't need proof of my worth. I had to prove it to the nation. I wouldn't risk discovering what the director thought I couldn't live without. The memory of his words sounded like he meant *people* I couldn't live without. I'd endure the assumptions and hatred from the other contestants to save the lives of the people I loved.

CHAPTER 14

Sleep never won me over. I spent the rest of the night in bed, legs tucked up to my chest, rocking back and forth. It was the best position for perseverating on the misery of life after my path deviated from what was Foretold. The only break from those thoughts was the memory of Vance's face so close to mine in the tree. How his expression had transformed to one I'd loved years ago.

On my way down to the foyer in the morning, I avoided all mirrors. I didn't need confirmation that I looked like a person who hadn't slept. Enough haunted my brain without adding a visual of my pale, drawn face framed in frizz.

I was the last one downstairs, exactly how I planned it, to avoid being alone with the agent on spy duty.

Most people shot smiles my way and called out friendly greetings. My stomach lurched in answer. They'd change their attitudes after I refused to help them anymore. No reason to make anyone's test harder by breaking the news right then. I forced myself to wave, though it came out limp and unconvincing.

Vance's auburn hair beckoned my gaze to the center of the room, so I studiously looked at only the edges. My head snapped to a standstill during my perusal of the perimeters—Em stood at the far side of the room, twirling her hair, nowhere near Vance.

The door to the testing room opened. Gone was the previous woman who had thirsted for my failure. In her place was a man older than my parents, hairline receding. He appraised us, but his attention slid to the nearby agent before skittering back to the relative safety of potential Seers. Was he nervous about the director's men?

That made two of us.

I entered the testing space near the rear of the crowd. After everyone spread along the back wall, I noted with some satisfaction the bowl of water, pieces of wax, ladles, and candles on the center table. A hand clasped me on the shoulder. The sudden pressure made me lurch to the side, and I looked back in alarm.

"Way to come through, Tallie," a girl said, smiling brightly.

"Yeah, thank you!" someone next to her added.

Nodding in meek recognition of their thanks, my heart pounded in my ears. I wasn't so dense about myself that I didn't recognize my intense craving for approval. How could I let all these people down?

"Hello, I'm Granger," the new man said. "Er, Granger Johannsen. For today's test, you will melt wax into a bowl of water and make a prediction based on what you see." Though he spoke to us, his stare bounced between the camera and the agent. "Divine the breaking news story in tonight's broadcast."

Had they already recorded the news, or would it be live? I never paid attention to the news. Once in the Oracus, I would know anything relevant before it happened, let alone before the radio reported it. If the news broadcast was yet to be determined, someone could meddle with the results.

Corruption had never occurred to me in the Oracus Test, assuming our infallible Seers would catch it before it happened. The clandestine meetings with the director skewed my brain in a different direction.

There was nothing to do but go ahead with the test.

My turn came fifth. The physical tasks of wax divining were habitual, not needing much attention. Tipping my ladle of viscous, just-melted wax, I concentrated on the beginning of tonight's news. My hand tilted and hovered the ladle over the bowl, eyes vigilant on where the wax hit the water's surface.

The answer left me gasping. My grip on the ladle's handle faltered, and the hot end of the metal utensil flopped against the tender skin of my inner wrist, searing it. I dropped the ladle, letting it clatter to the floor, and gripped my arm just under the quickly reddening mark.

Head swimming, chest uncomfortably tight, I walked to the table that held paper and pencils. The simple act of writing stretched the injured skin on my dominant wrist. Breathing through the pain, I wrote my answer:

Kentucky Nation declares Divination an abomination to state religion. Unrepentant Seers eradicated.

The paper shook in my hand as I delivered it to the test officiant. The sick, gnawing horror that gripped me when I read the wax hadn't let go. My predictions normally came with a sense or feeling that led me to conjure the meaning. This had been vastly different. Actual images like a movie screen had flashed through my mind. Seers being cuffed and jailed, ripped from their families. Riots and blockades at the Kentucky borders. Shots fired from the militia.

Director Hooper scared me, there was no doubting that, but at least he didn't mistreat Seers for a skill they were born with. His requests felt altogether more reasonable in the wake of that horrific perspective.

I studied the expressions of those who had completed the test before me. None looked as shaken as I felt. Either they could hide their emotions better than me, or they had received a watered-down version of the answer. More likely, they had the wrong answer altogether.

My attention peaked during Vance's turn, and I felt free to watch him as he focused on the test. His moods used to be so easy to interpret. I wondered if I would notice any reaction to the divination's answer.

His eyes flew up from the bowl of water. Straight to mine. His mouth parted and, though hard to tell from the back of the room, it looked a little like fear.

The next moment, he ripped his gaze away and shifted his face to neutral. He gave his answer to Granger and stalked back to the group. Ferocity coiled in each step, the only thing that belied his calm face—but that was ridiculous. The answer shouldn't have angered him. It wasn't like he was Foretold. He, and everyone in his life, wouldn't be in danger if Seerdom were to be eradicated here.

All the contestants could give it up. It wasn't their identity, their lone contribution to society.

The final contestant scrawled an answer that was far too short to be correct. In quick, shaky words, Granger gave us instructions to listen to the news broadcast. Those who failed would be escorted out of the dormitory soon after. He waved us out of the room, like shooing a swarm of gnats.

I hovered near the rear of the group, avoiding the others. In my hesitation, I caught a breathless stare Granger pinned on the gray-suited man who had shouldered his way into the room. The agent nodded once, and Granger let loose a long breath, dabbing at his forehead with the back of his hand.

I wasn't the only one under pressure.

Tucking my chin to my chest, I hustled to the door, only to be stopped by a firm hand on my shoulder. I gulped and risked a glance up. It was the agent.

"Remember. No failures." His voice was a fraction of a whisper, so similar to how my kidnapper sounded the night before. Maybe they were all trained in delivering sub-audible commands, but I suspected this was the same man.

I nodded, unable to make a sound through the nerves clogging my mind and my throat. He released me, but I would be incredibly stupid if I thought he wouldn't be watching to be sure I kept my word.

Ethyl waited for me in the foyer. Her eyes glinted with excitement. "Ready for another lesson? I gathered up all your sticks from yesterday, so you can figure out what tomorrow's test will be."

This is for my parents' lives, I reminded myself. *This is for our nation, that doesn't mistreat its Seers*. It all sounded noble, and I knew it was important, but putting my decision into practice felt like walking on spikes. I would crush dreams today and earn myself the hatred of every person waiting in the living room for my lesson. I couldn't make Ethyl deliver the bad news. She didn't deserve that.

I nodded, not wanting to lie out loud. Unable to say no and give an excuse I would have to repeat in a minute to everyone else. She didn't seem bothered by my less-than-enthusiastic reply and led the way down the hall.

I stopped short at the end of the hallway, in view of the living room. Every single contestant was there, waiting for me. Wanting to learn from me so they could have a fair shot to become a Seer, to elevate themselves and their families to Elite status.

I despised myself. Earnestly.

Through the crowded room, my eyes didn't rest until they landed on Vance. He stood next to Julion, behind a couch crammed with five people, one of them sitting on someone else's lap.

"I'm sorry," I started, knowing that part would be easiest—the words were habitual after the pressures of being Foretold.

I squeezed my eyes shut, willing the coming tears to stall. This would be better if they hated me. If they thought I was selfish, they would dismiss me and never speak to me again. That was the only way to ensure I wouldn't slip and tell someone about Director Hooper.

"For what?" Vance's voice carried across the room and sank into my chest like a knife.

I opened my eyes, facing my duty. "I can't teach you anything else." That wasn't enough. I had to say it differently, had to convince them. "I won't waste my time, so don't ask again."

The words felt so wrong. Vomit would have been more comfortable coming out of my mouth. Unable to stick around for the repercussions, I turned on my heel and fled down the hallway, only letting the tears fall when I reached the foyer.

A single nod from the agent was all that greeted me, and his approval made me feel so much worse. Turning away from him, I dashed to the front door and escaped outside.

"Tallie?"

I wiped my sleeve across my eyes. Carinne was standing on the sidewalk—a lifeline in the wreckage of my life. We barely knew each other, but she'd shown up for me again, right when I needed a friend.

"What happened?" she asked, rushing toward me.

I glanced backward, suddenly afraid an angry mob would erupt from the building, chasing me. "Can we walk and talk?" I croaked out between sniffles.

Carinne nodded and looped her arm through mine, so our elbows linked. She steered me back in the direction she had come from, and we rushed away from the dormitory.

CHAPTER 15

It was a long walk to the apprentice dormitory that had housed me for two nights before the competition. Carinne took me up to her room on the third floor. I couldn't call it my room anymore, though she hadn't gotten a new roommate.

She ate up every detail of my story, stopping me a few times so she could scribble in her notebook. Apparently, my life was inspiration fodder.

"Do you want to listen to the news here?" she offered. "The cafeteria has a radio."

"That's probably a good idea," I said, wondering if it would break an unspoken competition rule. Granger told us to listen to the broadcast but hadn't specified where.

Someone knocked on the door.

I scooted farther back on my old bed, putting useless distance between myself and the door.

Carinne shot me a look from behind her blonde side bangs and cracked the door open.

"Em?" I asked, blinking in shock.

She brushed past Carinne, flipping her long dark hair behind one shoulder. Carinne stood at the open door for a few affronted moments before huffing out a breath and easing it closed. Returning to her bed, she pulled a notebook onto her lap and opened it to a blank page. Her hand movements indicated sketching, rather than writing.

"I know what happened," Em said, standing in the middle of the room.

If it were me, I would have shrunk back to a wall, hugged my arms around my chest, or at least fidgeted. Em stood with nearly perfect posture; arms relaxed at her sides. I wondered what it was like to own her level of confidence, no matter where I was.

"Sorry, which thing that happened?" There had been so much, in so little time, it was impossible to guess what she referred to.

"Hooper threatened you into stopping the lessons," Em said. "He's a creep."

I shrugged, remembering the flashes of insight I had into Kentucky's nation. "He could be worse."

Em tilted her head at an elegant angle, staring down at me with raised eyebrows. "Your prediction was quite a show. It affected me, too, even second-hand."

How could she know that? Maybe she was like Adalia, the woman who tested the prospective contestants from my apprentice dormitory. I hadn't felt any thoughts getting sucked from my head, though. That wasn't an experience that could sneak by unnoticed.

"How do you know what I saw?" I asked.

"I can't read minds," she said, seeming to disprove her own statement. "I can see things that have already happened by concentrating on the person involved."

"You can see the past *and* divine the future?" I asked.

Carinne paused in her sketching, glancing up for the answer.

"Only the past," Em said. "I've been checking what answers people already gave while I pretend to complete the divination task. It's interesting to see the different interpretations, but so far, I've stuck with copying you."

No hint of apology for cheating. If I wasn't mistaken, she seemed proud, her eyes glinting as she held my gaze steadily. I'd never heard of a past-Seer, or whatever her talent would be called.

"So why are you here?" Carinne asked, after waiting through my silence.

Em kept her focus on me. "I might not like you, but what everyone's saying about you is untrue, and not quite fair. You deserve to know that not everyone thinks you're a stuck-up, lying bitch."

"I don't really need the *exact* words they're saying," I muttered, cringing away from the description.

"Oh, I left out the majority. That's just the most popular title. I'll spare you Julion's thoughts on the matter. But," she paused, pursing her lips in consideration, "do you want to hear what Vance had to say?"

I shook my head side-to-side forcefully. My cheeks flushed warm and bright, knowing Vance's girlfriend guessed my feelings for him. The humiliation was continuous and ever-growing.

"He was never my boyfriend, you know," she said.

"Are you sure you can't read minds?" I asked, only halfway joking.

She laughed. "Unnecessary. Any idiot could see the way you drool over him. You know he's not an idiot, but he seems oblivious to your crush."

Omen's asshole, this kept getting worse. My face would never regain its normal color. I could never show up at the competition dormitory again. I should have taken the director's initial suggestion and faded into obscurity when I had the chance.

"Anyway," she continued, "as long as I'm here giving you kind truths, I thought you'd be interested. He told me last night that it isn't going to happen between us anymore."

At the word "anymore," the confirmation that they'd been together, my heart sunk all the way into my stomach, sending it on a seasick voyage through troubled waters. She was so beautiful, so confident. It wasn't a mystery why she was Vance's type.

Swallowing down my heartache, I offered what little I could. "Do you want to stay and listen to the news here? We were just going to head down to the cafeteria."

Em shook her head. "Wasn't planning on tuning in. I already heard and saw it all from your prediction."

"But Granger said we had to listen," I protested.

She combed the fingers of one hand through her long, straight hair, letting it fall strand by strand back into place. "I'm not in the habit of doing what anyone tells me to. Later."

Em strode from the room, either not aware or not caring how her visit had affected me.

Carinne apparently agreed with my take. "Well, that was … a lot," she said. "Who's Vance?"

Did she have to start with *that* segment of the revelations? "Someone I was friends with a few years ago."

"Sounds like more than friends." Carinne crossed the room and sat next to me on my bed. She brought her notebook with her.

I took a peek at what she had been sketching. It was an exaggerated caricature of Em, a speech bubble over her head saying, *I'm so important, blah, blah, blah.*

"I wasn't supposed to be friends with him, but being a Foretold was a lot of pressure," I said, speaking that truth for the first time. No one else seemed to struggle with it like I did. No one else had the high marks I did, either. "When I was thirteen, I had my first panic attack. The more goals that were set for me, the more they came. But my parents were so proud of me, and our instructors kept telling me what a natural I was. My accomplishments were all anyone noticed about me. Nothing else about me mattered, so I worked harder, not wanting to let anyone down. But in my free time, I started running."

"Away?" Carinne asked with a hint of a smile.

I yielded a small laugh and shook my head. "No. Kind of? Anyway, I started going farther and farther, and one day, when I was fourteen, I was so distracted I literally ran into Vance. We both fell. He was fine, as always, but I was all scraped arms and bloody knees. Even though it was my fault, he was so careful with me, took me home to have his mom patch me up, making jokes the whole time to keep my mind off the scrapes. For the first time, my mind was off my Seerdom, and what I needed to be doing and achieving. I could *breathe.*

"The next day, I took the same route. I found his crew hanging out, just existing, not having the pressure to accomplish anything. It was …" I paused to shake my head, huffing out a breath of laughter. "It was the best. I kept coming around, and they eventually adopted me. They were all pretty cool, but no one was like Vance. He calmed my mind. And my heart."

Carinne let my cheesy wording slip by. "I don't think I've ever seen an Elite hanging out with Pedestrians before."

"There's no *rule*, but I really wasn't supposed to. My parents only ever had me. No other kids. My Foretelling gave them a lot to be proud of and they didn't want me to get thrown off course by," I choked out the words, "'aimless, worthless, destructive youth.'"

Carinne cringed and I remembered too late that she was a Pedestrian, lumped in with my parents' assumptions about Vance and his crew.

"I hung out with them for about a year before I got caught. My mom *screamed* at me. Not where anyone could hear, of course. My dad cried. Real tears. After that, they gave me lessons and presentations about the consequences of not becoming a Seer. I had to write an essay on every achievement I made in class as a Foretold, then another on the ideas of wastefulness and worth."

"Wow. That was very subtle of them," Carinne said.

I huffed a humorless laugh in agreement. "They made me promise to stay away from my friends. I had a huge crush on Vance by then and didn't want to let go. I wrote him a letter telling him how I felt and asking him to meet me that night."

Carinne waited, unmoving, holding her bangs back from her face with one hand so she could better see what was coming.

"He never showed. I waited all night. My parents found me around three in the morning, shivering and crying, insisting that I had to stay until he came." I shifted my eyes sideways at her, certain I was blushing. "I was fifteen. It was a lot."

She shook her head. "It's cool. You should've seen the poetry I wrote about my crush when I was that age. It was like four notebooks long and so cringy. Then he made out with my cousin, and I burned them all."

I nodded, remembering the swirling emotions that could take over at that age. Apparently, they could still take over at eighteen, because I was overwhelmed with relief that Vance didn't have a girlfriend, but also devastated that he'd been hanging out with a girl so far beyond my league that we were barely the same species. The way it had felt in the oak tree, staring into his eyes, I could have hung on that branch forever. Then the return of his coldness made me want to curl up in bed and never get out again. It couldn't be healthy. None of it.

"It's almost time for the news," Carinne said. "Want to go down early and get something to eat?"

I nodded, though my stomach didn't feel at all capable of digestion. Aside from everything about Vance, Em had blown open a whole new realm of possibility when it came to extra senses people could have. Between Adalia's thought stealing, Ethyl's lie scent, and now Em's past-Seer skill, I wondered how many people had abilities that were hidden away. People whose talents weren't appreciated or utilized like Seerdom was. Didn't they deserve as much recognition as Seers? There were myriad uses for those senses. Maybe Director Hooper didn't know about them.

Except his government had sent Adalia to search people's thoughts to determine if they had latent Seer talent or not, so he knew that skill existed. I couldn't decide why they wouldn't employ every ability. It was too much to detangle on the way to the cafeteria to listen to news about the persecution of people like me.

CHAPTER 16

Static crackled from the speakers as they caught the beginnings of the news broadcast.

"Former directorate employee turned national traitor, Adalia Carpenter, was apprehended this evening. She is being held for questioning in relation to tampering with the most recent Oracus entrance ceremony and working against the interests of the nation's newest event, the Oracus Test. More details after this breaking news."

Adalia. It couldn't be the same woman who had helped me get into the Oracus Test, could it? She'd been so intent on the veracity of Seers. Too loyal to be a traitor. I shook my head, dismissing the idea that she tampered with the entrance ceremony. More likely, the gate wards recognized me as some kind of fraud who didn't have actual talent. I just did more homework than any of my classmates. The broadcast announcer, done with his too-dramatic pause, broke through my thoughts.

"Kentucky Nation declares Divination an abomination to state religion. Unrepentant Seers eradicated."

The broadcast delved into the story details. A new law in Kentucky passed by a wide margin to outlaw Seer activities. Current and training Seers could renounce their talent and commit to a life of not using it. Those who didn't were arrested in high enough numbers they would rot in prison before their turn at a trial ever came. Some attempted to flee. Pedestrian citizens had taken it upon themselves to patrol Kentucky's northern border with Ohio. They confronted the runaway Seers, violently, leading to twenty-seven deaths, and many more injuries. According to Oracus' predictions, those numbers would continue to rise.

Laughter broke out two tables away from where Carinne and I sat.

"Seriously, didn't they know that was coming? Guess they're not so smart after all," one guy said, smirking like irritation was his favorite game.

"Serves them right," the guy next to him said, loud enough to catch the attention of the entire cafeteria.

Too many murmurs and shouts of agreement filled the space, joined by the clatter of my dropped fork as it fell to the floor. My heartbeat thundered between my ears, not quite drowning out the buzz of callous celebration. Did Pedestrians really hate Elites that much? Or just Seers? Carinne's face filled with pity, but I wondered if she felt the same way the others did. She wasn't saying anything to stick up for me.

I shoved away from the table.

"Tallie," Carinne said.

I cut her off with a raised hand. "Sorry, I have to go. I'm sorry," I said, and fled the cafeteria, then the building.

It felt like I had done nothing but run away ever since the failed Oracus ceremony. In truth, I'd been running away a lot longer than that, just from something different. From the pressure to be exactly who everyone said I was, and to do it well enough to keep my parents' heads held high.

The apprentice dormitory was close to the Oleski home. I could use a good dose of Gina. As I neared their house, I wondered if she and the rest of the family shared the same negative view of Elites. Perhaps I had accidentally made them feel inferior at some point, too. All the more reason to visit. While none of the strangers at the apprentice dormitory would care about an apology from me, Gina and her family would be receptive. I couldn't let everyone everywhere hate me, even if I deserved it.

My pace picked up to a swift jog, bordering on a run. It felt good, something I hadn't done in too long, but I reached the Oleski's house before my lungs could truly burn. A silver car idled on the street. The evening had grown dusky enough that I could see into the bright front window of the house. Their kitchen was occupied by two men with shaved heads, both wearing the gray suits specific to the director's agents. Vance's father stood in front of them, red faced and bristling. Gina sat behind him at the table. Something looked terribly wrong about her, like a balloon that had sat for too many days, leaking air through an invisible pinprick.

The men must have finished whatever errand they were on because they disappeared from the window and appeared outside the house. It happened faster than I could hide.

One agent pointed a long arm at me and the other turned his head directly to where I stood.

Run, my thoughts commanded, but my body stalled. Director Hooper scared me, but he just wanted the Seers to continue functioning. I couldn't fault him for that. Instead of surrendering to the impulse to flee, I planted my feet and waved. A stupid little gesture. It wasn't like one of the director's agents would break from intimidation mode to *wave back* at me.

The second man approached and herded me toward the car. Before being shoved inside, I glanced back at the Oleski's house, craning my neck for one last look inside. Vance's dad had sunk into one of the kitchen chairs and propped his elbows on the table. He dropped his head into his hands. My stomach clenched in fear, worrying something had gone wrong with Liann. Their family didn't deserve any type of tragedy.

After a less-than-gentle shove, I stumbled into the empty backseat. I buckled up and wondered if it was worth my time asking a question to the silent suits.

"Why were you looking for me?" I asked anyway.

"You can't be trusted. No more running off," the driver said.

I couldn't be trusted. The insult burned away at my insides like unjust accusations tended to do. I let down every person in the Oracus Test, exactly like the director wanted, and he still didn't trust me.

The rest of the drive passed in silence. Theirs was professional. I spent mine stewing, wondering how I could gain more trust. Being confined to the competition dormitory was low on my list of things to look forward to—everyone there hated me.

They didn't drop me off outside the building. Both agents exited the car and escorted me inside like a prisoner. There weren't any other agents in the dormitory, clinching the notion that their presence was to observe me, not for general contestant security.

They waited at the bottom of the stairs until I reached the second floor. I breathed a sigh of relief that no one was in the hallway. Not wanting to push my luck, I rushed to my room.

Ethyl was there, hugging a book to her chest. She was flanked by Kinsley and one other girl. Kinsley perched next to her, patting her back, and the other sat on the floor, reclining against the bedframe.

The one on the floor was in the middle of speaking when I entered.

"Some people can't handle competition. Especially not an Elite. They're used to having everything just handed to them."

She stopped when she realized I had entered the room. Kinsley took up where she left off, staring daggers at me.

"It's not your fault for trusting her, Ethyl. Maybe Kentucky had the right idea."

It was hard to breathe, but I drew in enough air to push out a quick, "Sorry."

"Don't bother. Just get out," Ethyl said.

All three girls glared at me with their arms crossed. Ethyl's eyes were rimmed with red. I ached to tell them that it wasn't my choice. But the agents would find out, they would report it to Director Hooper, and I'd be treated to another midnight kidnapping, with far worse results.

Hanging my head, I gathered the pillow and blanket off my bed and left the room. I hovered in the hallway, just outside the door. Where to sleep? The living room was out. Chances were too high that someone was hanging out in there. There was a long bench in the dining room, but again, too high-traffic of a location. Maybe I could sleep on the floor at the end of the hallway. I walked to the end farthest from the stairs, considering the feasibility. Comfort was off the table. My hope was for a horizontal surface and relative quiet.

Tense male voices erupted from the right-hand room at the end of the hall:

"Admit it, she's shady as hell. Just let her go, man."

"I already did. Three years ago, I let her go. What else does anyone want from me?"

Vance. Omen's asshole, Julion and Vance were arguing, and it had to be about me. I could stay and listen, maybe find out some of Vance's reasons for leaving me hanging, or I could give them their privacy and get out of there.

"But you didn't, really. It's your life, but she did a number on you, man. You let the hottest girl here get away over it."

"Watch your mouth, Julion."

"What? You ditched Em the minute you played hero in the tree with Tallie. You think Hudson didn't tell everyone about that?"

"I said, drop it," Vance's voice dropped into a low register I didn't recognize.

I couldn't even picture what he would look like barely keeping it together.

Waiting in the hallway, listening, hadn't been a conscience decision, but I couldn't talk my legs into taking me away.

"You're probably in the competition to get on her level. Maybe you'll finally be good enough once you're an Elite, right?"

I'd never witnessed a fight, but the sound of a fist hitting flesh was unmistakable. Ditching my pillow and blanket on the floor, I lunged for the doorknob and let myself into the room.

Julion was righting himself from where he had sprawled on his bed, one hand holding his blood-smeared nose and upper lip.

Vance stood close by, shaking out his fist. His eyes were wide, shocked, but his words came out resolute. "I need to be Elite because my mom is sick. She needs better care, so I have to try. How was I supposed to know Tallie would be here, messing everything up?"

I gasped. My hands flew to cover my mouth, but it was too late to slip away unnoticed.

Vance and Julion both whipped their heads around to face me. Julion looked like he wanted to say something, but after a glare from Vance, thought better of it.

"Your mom," I said, stepping toward Vance. "I had no idea. I'm so sorry, she—"

"Yeah, you're sorry, Tallie?" Vance spent more time on the word sorry than he did on my name, and the difference sent my stomach roiling. "You're always so sorry, but never for the things you should be." He stormed past me and out of the room.

Glancing at Julion, I decided it would be better for me to leave, too.

By the time I got into the hallway, Vance was nowhere to be seen. I would have gone after him, would have asked him what I needed to apologize for, but he clearly didn't want to be around me. He said I was messing everything up. It wasn't a surprise. I knew that as deeply as I knew anything. All I did anymore was mess things up, for myself and everybody else.

I snatched my pillow and blanket from the floor, then trudged downstairs to the foyer, where I ignored the agent standing guard. I wasn't going to do anything *untrustworthy*, so I had nothing to worry about from him. In fact, I'd be free from all government suspicion for the night, because I would spend it in one of the foyer's chairs, in full view of the director's spy. They wanted me to win the competition, so they wouldn't let any angry contestants keep me awake, ranting at me or insulting me.

I dropped my pillow against the wooden arm of the oversized straight-back chair, wishing I was brave enough to ask the agent to relocate to the living room. If he watched over me there, I could at least have a couch. At the moment, though, I didn't deserve to ask anything from anybody.

Sitting on the chair with a sigh I couldn't control, I pulled my knees up to my chest and turned sideways. Resigned to discomfort, I pulled the blanket up, tucked it all the way under my chin, and closed my eyes.

"What are you doing?"

I opened one eye to see the agent squinting at me, upper lip curled in a grimace.

"Sleeping," I replied, too weary to apologize for my presence.

I didn't sleep, or at least, not right away. I stayed in that chair for hours with my eyes closed, pretending, but my mind was far too wild and away for sleep to come. Foremost in my thoughts was the worry about Gina, and how long Vance had known she was sick. I didn't know if it was serious, but his presence in the competition told me it was. Gina was the backbone of that family. They couldn't suffer her loss. If only there was a way to ensure that Vance was the other winner at the end of this all. Then his mom would receive the best care at the nation's top hospital.

From history class, abstractly, I knew hospitals used to treat thousands of patients a day before the separation of states. Now, supplies, resources, staff, everything was restricted, so decisions had to be made. Priorities chosen. Since the Seers were essential to the running of the nation, they and their families had first dibs on medical care. I still remembered seeing Vance's neighbor from down the street when I was fourteen. The grocery store had kicked him out, and he had shoved over stands and thrown a rock through their window, in a rage because they stopped carrying the food he needed for his diabetic kid.

I remembered watching, horror-stricken, at the man's violent outburst. I had asked Vance why he needed special food so much, and why he couldn't just get the insulin dose changed. Bryla, my Foretold friend, was diabetic, and she ate almost anything she wanted thanks to her insulin shots. Vance had kicked around a rock on the sidewalk, looking like he might pick it up and help the angry man. He'd told me they didn't have any medicine and wouldn't get any. It all went to the Elites. I had felt sick at the dawning knowledge. Still did.

Sometimes, being able to predict future events seemed useless in the face of present misery.

Nothing about my ability could help Gina. I could only see what would happen, not how to make it better.

CHAPTER 17

I woke to a sharp nudge on my arm. My eyes squinted against the interruption until the nudge turned into a poke that jabbed deeper.

I opened my eyes into slits. Em stared down at me, looking less than pleased to be on wake-up duty.

"You look homeless," she said, a faint wrinkle marring her dainty nose.

"I am homeless," I replied. I had no idea where my parents moved to. I wasn't an apprentice, so I didn't have a right to my shared room with Carinne. Ethyl had kicked me out of our room.

"Well, it's sad. And distracting." Her voice lacked any emotion that would back up her words. "The last of my roommates got sent home last night, so if you don't have anywhere else, take one of their beds."

Maybe I was still dreaming. Or stuck in a bleary early-morning hallucination. Em was asking me to move into her room? That was bound to be uncomfortable, but perhaps not as bad as sleeping in a straight-back chair in sight of an intimidating man in a directorate-issued gray suit.

"Yeah, um, okay. Thank you."

"We're not friends or anything," Em tossed back. She was already heading for the stairs.

I scrambled to my feet but was more tangled in my blanket than I realized and crashed straight to the floor. I didn't want to know if Em stopped to wait for me to recover, or if the agent reacted at all. There wasn't a chance I would make eye contact with anybody after that move. Taking my time, I disentangled my limbs from the blanket and sat up to fold it carefully into a small rectangle before standing up again.

Vance hovered in the doorway. Like me, he held a blanket tucked under one arm. It looked like he had spent the night in the living room. We were so close while sleeping, and for some reason that made my cheeks burn with an unforgiving blush.

"We're going to my room," Em announced to him from her spot three stairs up. "Looks like you could use a place to stay, too. Want to join? Wouldn't be the first time you slept there." She rolled her hips to the side as she spoke, adjusting herself into a pose I could never dream of replicating.

Omen's asshole, I was on my way to move into a room where they had spent the night together. The foyer chair grew in appeal as burning shame assaulted my insides.

"Stop, Em," Vance said, in a tone eerily similar to the one he'd used with Julion the night before. "It's not funny."

"Really? I thought it was." Em laughed in an oddly carefree way, then started up the stairs again. "Come on, Tallie."

Go with the girl who didn't like me and had just propositioned my long-time crush, or stay in the foyer with an unpredictably moody version of that crush? Sighing, I picked the option with less potential for devastation and trudged up the stairs after Em. She led me down the hallway until we reached the end and she turned to the left-hand door. Directly across from Vance and Julion's room.

"You're staying across the hall from him?" I asked in more of a squeak than a human voice.

"Mm-hmm," she replied casually, then let us into her room.

Four twin beds were crammed into a space that would have comfortably fit three. She gestured to one bed, and I set my pillow and blanket on it. I'd have to get the rest of my stuff out of Ethyl's room. Maybe I could be late for the next test; do it when the room was empty.

Now that my hands were free, I looked around for something to do with them. Being in Em's personal space, knowing what had happened in there, my body and mind were completely off balance.

"Relax," Em said. "I was joking earlier with Vance."

"Why?" I asked, completely clueless as to why she would stir the pot that way.

She shrugged. "Sometimes I do whatever will get the biggest reaction just to see how people react. With everyone out there who can tell the future before it happens, it's fun to shake things up. Maybe make them wrong every once in a while. Not that any Seers are wasting their time predicting what happens in my boring life."

It wasn't the answer I expected. I thought there would be pining over Vance, maybe some pettiness, but she seemed as far from reactionary as humanly possible. A wave of envy washed over me that had nothing to do with Vance and everything to do with a deep desire to control my anxiety when it struck. To witness things around me and not be rendered incapacitated if they were upsetting. I swallowed down the jealousy. Even if it was unconventional, she had done a nice thing for me.

"Thank you, for giving me a place to stay."

"Seriously, don't mention it." She flipped her hair over one shoulder. "Gratitude is weird. I'm going to grab breakfast."

Something she said the day before popped into my mind. Who knew if she'd continue being so forthcoming? It might be my only chance to ask.

"Em?"

She didn't reply but stopped on her way to the door.

"You said you didn't like me, aside from the Seerdom," I said. "Why is that?"

She remained facing away from me, speaking to the door. "I've never learned not to look." She shook her head slowly. "Everyone has a past. Past crushes, hook-ups, whatever. But I've always hoped I could be someone's first love. So, I look into guys' pasts when I get involved, hoping I won't find anything serious. The way Vance looked at you, it was … I never felt ashamed of seeing anyone else's past before, but I felt *gross* like some weird stalker or something, spying on a person's private time that no one else was supposed to see. He turned his whole life to orbit around you. It doesn't need to be him, but I want someone to look at me that way."

As I stood, stricken and stuck in place, Em hurried from the room, her typical swagger morphing into something closer to a jog.

"I'm sorry," I whispered to her absence.

She thought I was an obstacle to her having a relationship with Vance. Little did she know, he didn't want anything to do with me.

Maybe he had cared about our friendship, but I'd seen him with his parents, his sisters, his friends. He treated everyone he cared about like they were important. I wasn't different from any of them, back when we were friends.

Even as I excused every assumption she made about his past, hope implanted its stubborn self into my welcoming, wanting heart.

CHAPTER 18

Eighteen contestants gathered in the testing room. Five arrows and a rudimentary wooden bow rested on the table in front of us. A small target hung on one side wall. Granger presided over the scene, his chest puffed and eyes only for the camera, almost a different man from the previous day.

"Another nation has banned Seers and their ilk," he said. "Details will be broadcast tonight, but a select few, including myself, have already been informed. For your test, I have written the name of one nation on each arrow shaft. Your task is to read the names, shoot all five arrows, and make your prediction from where they land. Natalie Kowalczyk, please step forward. You are the first to be tested on which nation will be named in tonight's broadcast."

This form of belomancy had always been my favorite. Something about releasing the arrow and hearing the satisfying thunk of it sinking into a bullseye eased my tension. I picked up the first arrow, reading the nation's name printed in small letters along the shaft.

New England. I read the rest: Ohio, Arizona, Missibama, and Carolina. Other than the writing, the arrows were identical. I held onto New England and set the others down.

"One more thing," Granger interrupted. "After your turn is complete, you are to exit to the foyer, not speaking a word to anyone on the way out. Anyone caught cheating, or under suspicion of cheating, will be disqualified from potential Seerdom. Only trustworthy individuals may enter the Oracus."

A few laughs and indiscernible comments ran through the crowd behind me, but I caught one.

"Trustworthy?" Ethyl said. "She's disqualified."

More laughter.

I closed my eyes and breathed deeply and slowly. I tuned out the distractions and focused on which nation was next to eradicate Seers. The space of prediction was the only arena where I could ignore my thoughts, like how hated I had become. And worse, the arrests and deaths from the night before.

I positioned the arrow against the bow and pulled the string back. Rather, I tried to pull it back. The bow was tighter than those I had used at school, and my arm shook against the tension. Being Foretold, knowing my strength lay in my mind, not my limbs, I had never wasted time feeling embarrassed about my upper body weakness. If I didn't win the Oracus Test, that would change. I relaxed my arm and let the string fall back into place and set the bow and arrow back on the table. Clenched each fist, just once, then relaxed my hands. I grabbed the bow and arrow once more, gritted my teeth while I positioned the arrow, pulled back in one swift yank, and released.

The arrow's tail snagged against my hand that held the bow and fell to the floor, inches in front of me.

The laughter was wider spread that time.

They didn't know how decisively I had eliminated one nation from the running. Faltering, failing arrows were much better than if each one hovered around the bullseye, making an accurate prediction almost impossible.

I reached back to the table and selected the Missibama arrow. I repeated the process. This arrow struck the outer rim of the target. I frowned. That wasn't ideal. Either it would be the answer, but uncertain, or there would be other answers competing for which would be most likely.

The next two arrows fell limply to the floor, not far from the first. Each time, the other contestants laughed—a reminder that they didn't understand what was happening. *That* sent the guilt running rampant. They should have known what was happening. If I hadn't let them all down, I would've spent the previous day teaching them the nuances of belomancy.

One arrow to go. I shook off the intrusive thoughts, commanded my tired arm to *keep it together* and let the final arrow loose. It split the very air around it in a straight course for the bullseye, where it buried itself decisively.

That would be the answer then. I set the bow down on the table and met Granger at the target, resisting the urge to rub my shaking bicep. I pulled the arrow from the bullseye, watched him read the name—*Ohio*—then ensured he wrote it correctly on his sheet. Yielding to curiosity, I double-checked the arrow that had landed on the edge of the target. The nation of Missibama. A shiver of foreboding ran through me, but I hustled out of the room with my eyes trained on the floor. I couldn't give anyone a reason to accuse me of sharing the answer. Since the possibility of cheating was introduced, the more ambitious contestants might eliminate the competition with accusations, false or not.

I continued my fast pace through the foyer, up the stairs, and into Ethyl's room. I picked up the cardboard box holding my belongings, and, after bumping into the doorframe twice, fled to Em's room. After living in the same house for half of my life, being shuttled from one dormitory to the next made it difficult to think of this latest space as "my room." Attachment wasn't wise when I was a step away from being homeless. Sure, I had shelter, a roof over my head, but nothing was *mine* and none of it was guaranteed.

I dropped the box with a thud, shook out my trembling arms, then sat on the bed I had claimed as my temporary sleeping space. That was as committed to the place as I could let myself get.

Eighteen contestants remained. After today, the number would dwindle dramatically. This type of belomancy would be impossible to make it through with luck. People without Seer abilities would just be shooting arrows, and the answers would be meaningless. The truth wouldn't soar in its own pursuit of the bullseye. If they had good aim, they could hit the bullseye, but they might do so with every arrow, no matter which was correct.

Or they could be miserable shots, and miss each one, without even an arrow sticking from the very edge of the target to pass as an answer.

Today would reveal who had a true Seer talent and who had coasted by with luck. My mind flashed to Gina's drawn face, illuminated in her kitchen window. Vance needed to pass today's test and all the others. Gina couldn't suffer through something treatable. I hoped it was treatable.

A light knock on the door broke me from my thoughts.

"Come in?" I asked, uncertain of the rules when alone in somebody else's room.

The door opened slowly, and familiar auburn hair atop a chiseled diamond face appeared. I wanted to vomit.

"Em's not here," I told him.

Vance walked in and closed the door behind him. "I know."

Oh. He was there for me. My heart sped to an unsustainable pace as he sat on the unclaimed bed between Em's and mine. I forbade my brain from conjuring what his other visits to this room would have looked like.

He leaned forward, resting his elbows on his thighs. Had his eyes been that tired all along?

"You don't have to stay here," he said.

"Yes, I do. I need to finish the competition." What was he talking about? He didn't understand how deeply my sense of self had been buried when the Oracus had denied me entry.

Worried, furrowed eyebrows lowered over his stare that stole my breath. "I mean this room. You don't have to stay with Em if it's uncomfortable. She has a way of making people say yes, even if they don't want to."

The nausea returned. "I guess it makes sense that you wouldn't want me here," I said, desperately trying to keep my emotions in check. I was close to crying, but equally close to lunging across the small space and demanding why he left me hanging three years ago.

Vance tipped his head back and sighed. He stared at the ceiling for the longest minute I had ever survived before leveling his gaze back at me. "I know you heard me say you're messing everything up."

I nodded, not sure any possible reply would be welcome. But the words came out anyway, a reflex ingrained as deeply as breathing. "I'm sorry."

Vance reached a hand across the narrow space between beds and put it on top of mine.

I froze. If I moved, he would move, and that brief touch would be over.

"Tallie," he said, taking his time with the first syllable and stalling my heart. "Breathe, please."

"I am," I whispered, still not moving. And, fine, not breathing either.

"Then why are you turning so red?"

"Other reasons," I choked out with the last of the air in me, forcing me to inhale noisily.

Vance smiled to one side and took his hand back. I *knew* he would move if I did.

"What I meant to say is that I'm messing up plenty on my own. I can't believe I hit Julion." He scoffed, halfway between a laugh and a groan. "Omen's asshole, it should have been anybody but him. I can't decide what's worse—that I hit someone or that you saw."

The words Vance spoke when I burst onto the scene came back to me. He was overcome with emotion about his mom being sick. I was worried about her, too. It was time to stop obsessing over what hadn't happened between Vance and me.

"Can you tell me about your mom? She seemed like her normal self when I saw her before the competition."

Vance squeezed his eyes shut and ran his tongue over his teeth behind his closed lips. He opened his eyes but kept them trained on his lap, where his hands were clasped. "It's cancer."

The word sat heavy and oppressive in the space between us.

"She has good days and bad days. The good days outnumber the bad, but there's no chemotherapy available for her. Only palliative junk that doesn't do a thing to cure it."

"Oh, Vance," I said, my voice thick with sadness. No wonder he entered the Oracus Test. He had probably broken up with Em to concentrate on winning. "Is there anything I can—that I can do?"

"Unless you ditched becoming a Seer because you're a doctor now? No. But Liann told me your visit was a good distraction for Mom. Thanks for seeing her. She, ah," he rubbed the back of his neck and the tips of his ears reddened, "she missed you."

"I missed her, too," I said, meaning it more deeply than words could convey. This was no time to specify that I'd missed him most of all. That time would never come.

The relaxed attitude he'd had since entering the room faded, replaced with the icy stranger I'd seen in the past few days. The change was sudden, and I felt it like a knife in my gut.

"You didn't *have* to miss her." He stood with stiff, robotic movements. "I just wanted to tell you not to let Em push you around. And, uh, you don't have to worry about me punching anyone else. I haven't changed that much."

"Vance?" His name broke into two syllables in my desperate cry.

He turned around, thawing for a quick moment that shone with vulnerability, and hope, and …

My imagination was running wild. Still, I had to ask. "What answer did you give? For the test?"

"Ohio," he said, expression shuttering closed. He walked out, closing the door behind him.

Vance had the ability. He should have been Foretold.

It could be us at the end of it all.

CHAPTER 19

Thanks in part to courage and in larger part to Em's taunting version of encouragement, I joined everyone in the living room for the news broadcast. Two of the director's agents were present—one who remained in the foyer and one who leered, vulture-like, over the crowd in the living room.

Drawn-out static heralded the broadcast. "Ohio becomes the next Nation to declare Seers an enemy to the government. Detention centers erected in Cincinnati already stand at half capacity as fearful Seers turn themselves in to authorities."

My mouth hung open; silent tears trickled down my face. One stream skirted the edge of my mouth, tainting my senses with salted despair.

Half of the room erupted. Groans of frustration, heads hung, and a few tears shed. It was a world of difference from listening to the broadcast about Kentucky in the apprentice cafeteria. Maybe seeing into the Seer process these past few days helped the others gain sympathy for people like me. They were grieving this injustice.

The agents moved through the room in swift, precise movements, urging certain contestants to stand and exit the room. One by one, they headed for the door, and I realized it was everyone who had reacted to the news about Ohio.

The tenuous feeling of belonging and being understood shuttered itself away, deep inside. No one cared that Seers had been rounded up and jailed. They cared about losing a contest and not reaching Elite status.

One boy paused in front of me on his way out of the room. "I hope you lose," he spat out, eyes narrowed.

"You don't deserve to be here," the boy behind him agreed. "Stuck-up bitch."

A flash of movement caught my eye, and in the next second, Vance appeared between us.

"Get over it and get out," he said, taking up my field of vision with his broad upper back and tensed shoulders.

One agent raised an eyebrow at Vance but continued silently herding out the people who had failed.

"Ooh, Vance, hero mode looks good on you," Em called from across the room where she sat on a couch between Ethyl and Julion. "How could she resist?"

"I'm not saving anyone. I just don't like sore losers," Vance grumbled, retreating across the room.

Em cackled, openly enjoying messing with the atmosphere. But beside her, after Vance spoke, Ethyl grimaced and plugged her nose.

There were nine contestants left. Nine people who had predicted via belomancy. My mind rifled through the different assisted divination methods, wondering what would come with the next test. I didn't dare pick up the discarded pile of sticks to predict it. I had gone the whole night without being kidnapped by a single government entity and hoped to make that a habit. No need to rouse their suspicion just to satisfy my curiosity.

After Vance's protective maneuver, none of the other contestants took so much as a sideways glance at me. Neither did he. I still couldn't leave the dormitory due to the careful watch of the agents but at least I was trapped in a less hostile environment. I avoided being alone with Em, not wanting to hear her take on what happened after the broadcast, and fell asleep early.

It was still dark when someone shook me awake. My body reacted immediately, and I rolled away from the touch, off the side of the bed, and crashed onto the floor. Heart pounding, I ignored my sore butt and started scooting under the bed frame, making it harder for any agents to grab me.

"You're interesting to wake up," Em said, peering down at me. "I might do this every night."

"I thought you were someone else," I said, panting. After my breathing calmed, I eased out from the cramped space under the bed and stood up, wide awake. "What are you doing?"

"The guy running the tests just knocked. Said there's a storm brewing and we're doing the next test now. Whatever that means."

Astrapomancy. With untrained, unprepared, possibly not even Seers?

"We're going to make predictions from the lightning," I said.

"Through a window, or …" Em trailed off.

"Or," I confirmed her unspoken option. "It only works in the storm."

She gently bobbed her head from side to side, her long hair fluid with the movement. "Could be fun. Ready to go?"

From the looks of it, she had never gone to sleep. She wore the same clothes she had on earlier, and her hair lay smooth and straight. I glanced down at my baggy nightshirt.

"Sorry, not quite."

Em laughed. "I know. See you down there." She flounced out of the room, leaving the door open.

With a sigh, I walked to the doorway to close it, just as Vance and Julion left their room across the hall. A distant rumble of thunder prodded the air with its low vibration. Vance noticed me immediately. His eyes flicked down to my bare legs, hesitating there for a moment before making their way back up to my face. A chill traveled along the path of his gaze, and I jumped back, slamming the door shut. I leaned my forehead against it to catch my breath, then hurried to get dressed. I ran a brush through my hair twice before bolting out the door and rushing to the foyer.

Forcing myself into a sedate pace as I neared the bottom of the stairs, I searched the room for Vance. I didn't have any business being excited to see him, but I couldn't deny how I wanted him to look at me like that again.

The first droplets of rain splatted against the foyer windows; full, heavy drops that made themselves known upon impact. I had pawed through my box upstairs, but my parents hadn't packed a jacket for me.

Granger clapped his hands together one time when he saw me arrive. He turned to the lone camera, giving a hand signal to the woman operating it.

"Once the storm begins, so does the test. Tonight, these young hopefuls will use lightning to predict the future." He stared into the lens as he spoke, and I imagined him practicing his most dramatic face beforehand. He turned to us. "You will all interpret it simultaneously, in silence, then I will call you one at a time to write your prediction."

Eight people in the room crowded to the windows, looking into the night. I held back, waiting for the first flash. Claiming the front row at the window wouldn't do any good. We needed to be in the rain, surrounded by thunder, feet on the same earth that the lightning hit in order to comprehend the message in its strikes.

"Predict the reported number of people that perish on the first day of the next Seerdom ban," Granger said from behind us.

It was as if the first lightning strike didn't happen outside but in my body. They knew another ban was coming and that people would die. Had they analyzed trends and planted spies for inside information? Or was it an official Seer prediction? My mind flashed back to the arrow shaft bearing the name Missibama that had struck the edge of the target. There were only five nations represented in the last test, but the feeling stuck with me—it would be the next to make Seerdom illegal. This could be a trick question, and the answer was zero deaths in Missibama. I hoped with everything in me that it would be zero.

The Oracus Test didn't work that way. With the question in mind, I made my way to the door.

"Excuse me, sorry," I said, as I slipped between Em and another contestant whose name I didn't know. I stepped outside and into the falling rain.

Before the door closed behind me, I heard Kinsley ask, "What's she doing? The lightning hasn't even started yet."

Again, the guilt hammered into me. I knew what to do, and none of the others had that base knowledge. Being out in the storm that would produce lightning helped attune the body to the charge in the air. More time spent in a product of the storm clouds, getting soaked by their rain, took my mind closer to what the lightning would tell me when it arrived.

I stepped away from the building, avoiding the shelter of the oak tree. Raising my face to the sky, I let the large drops pelt my skin and drench my hair and clothes. I stretched my arms out to the side and spread my fingers.

Movement flashed in my periphery. Vance positioned himself just a couple of feet away with rain-darkened hair. I couldn't see a single hint of red. He copied my pose, greeting the storm face first and looking so gloriously alive I burned from the inside out. He turned from the clouds to point his wild grin at me, and it spread to my face, unstoppable. I laughed out loud at the sudden weightlessness of my body as the drops grew larger and fell faster. He threw his head back and beat his fists against his chest with an animalistic yell into the dark, wet night, making me laugh even harder. He cast me a triumphant, beaming look.

The scene illuminated, as bright as day, for a third of a second, and Vance's auburn strands gleamed. The lightning had arrived.

I tore my gaze away from my favorite color to focus on the heart of the storm before us, waiting for the next strike. I pushed the test and the question to the front of my mind, and the thought of dead Seers sobered the moment. Two seconds after the lightning struck, a crack of thunder filled the air. The storm was close, maybe too close. As a Foretold, I had practiced astrapomancy at a distance— accepting diluted predictions in exchange for safety. My classmates and I had gained the skill and the experience without risking injury or death.

I shot a fast, blurred look around and behind me. All the contestants were outside. The elation of seconds ago had vanished from Vance's face, replaced by pressed lips and a furrowed brow. He was worried. Rightly so.

I forced my gaze to the clouds. Blocked out everything but the Seers who would die in the next round of bans. I saw the millisecond it charged in the clouds. A flash of lightning took rapid, staggered steps down to the earth, then disappeared as fast as it had started.

One measly second, then the crashing, rumbling thunder assaulted my ears and rattled my chest. It was too close. The storm was *too close,* but one flash hadn't given me a full sense of the future.

Sooner than anticipated, another bolt shot from the sky, near enough that I wanted to close my eyes against its brightness. I couldn't waste the chance to read the lightning. Breathless at its severe beauty, momentarily deafened by thunder that rolled out behind it, I memorized the form and feel of the lightning strike. Unable to ignore my fear any longer, I turned and ran back to the building.

To each person I passed, I called out encouragement to follow me. I didn't care whether Granger or the agents would consider that cheating or not. It was too dangerous to be outside. I'd received the sternest lecture of my whole Foretold training on the day I first learned astrapomancy. "An electrocuted Seer is no use to the nation," the instructor had said.

As I reached the building, each individual hair on my arms rose. The door flew open, pushed from the inside by Granger, and I leaped into the building. As the door shut, I whipped around to watch the next bolt of lightning strike the ground, close enough to see the actual point—too close to Ethyl.

It didn't strike her body. It hit the dirt, maybe ten feet away, but she stiffened to complete immobility for a breathless second. Then she dropped to the ground and didn't move.

I strained my eyes in the pitch darkness that came after the blinding light but couldn't make out any details. I didn't know if thunder answered the bolt. The pounding of my heart filled my ears.

Julion pulled the door open, and Vance rushed in, holding a smoking, lifeless Ethyl.

He laid her on the floor, breathing too heavily to speak. The other contestants ran inside, pale and dripping. Silence descended over the group until Julion cursed and pushed past the others to Ethyl's side.

He dropped to his knees, pressed an ear to her chest, and shook his head. One hand over the other, he pumped up and down on her chest. He counted in a panting rhythm and paused at thirty to tilt her chin forward and breathe into her mouth twice before returning to the chest compressions. Though winded from carrying her, Vance took over giving the breaths at Julion's direction.

They continued like that for an eternity until Julion sat back on his heels and motioned for Vance to stop. They stayed next to Ethyl, watching and waiting. I stared at her chest, skin visible through her singed and hole-ridden shirt. There was no rise and fall. She was dead.

No one spoke or moved for the longest time. Then Kinsley, Ethyl's roommate, covered her face with her hands and sobbed—

quiet at first, then choking and gasping, her shoulders shaking. Julion rose haltingly to his feet. He looked around the room until his gaze landed on Granger's trembling form.

"So, do we add one extra to our death prediction?" he deadpanned.

Em stepped forward without hesitation and slapped his cheek, sending his head whipping to the side with a sharp crack. He paused, breathed, then turned to face her, skin already red and rising.

"Sorry," he said. "It's what I do when I don't want to feel shit. I … tried. I put everything I had into getting her back, but—" his eyes darted to Granger and the agent. "CPR can only do so much."

To my knowledge, Julion had never apologized in his life. It only took someone's death.

Ethyl's death. Staring at her felt wrong but looking anywhere else in the room felt worse. I settled on her face, trying to remember how it looked when she was so excited to learn divination. Her "smell test" was something unique and precious. I had never heard of that ability, and now it was lost along with her.

"Well, now, that was …" Granger tried making a statement, but trailed off, looking like he had just woken up somewhere different from where he'd fallen asleep. He looked at the agent. "What do we do now?"

The agent's nostrils flared; his only visible reaction that I had noticed so far. "Wait for the storm to settle, then call a disposal team. Until then, gather the predictions."

My mouth dropped open. They were going to make us finish the test after one of us *died*?

Belatedly, I noticed the camerawoman was no longer recording.

"Right, yes, obviously, that is what we will do," Granger said, adjusting the collar of his shirt. He glanced down at the paper in his hand and blinked several times before appearing to focus on it. "Em McEwen. Please enter the testing room to write down your answer."

Em couldn't go first. She'd been relying on other people's answers that were already written and submitted. It wasn't a Seer's ability, but it was incredible in its own right. The Oracus could help develop her past sight and use it for the greater good. As much as I yearned for the place I had lost among the Foretold, I couldn't let Em get eliminated. She might never get another chance to show what she could do. Steeling my spine, I hurried to step in front of her, cutting off her path.

I turned to Granger. "I'd like to go first," I said, fighting to rid my voice of its waver halfway through the demand.

"It's not up to you," the officiant said. He waved Em forward.

That couldn't happen. She would fail. Her talent deserved recognition. Legitimacy. To help her, I had to become her, just long enough to sell the attitude. A shudder ran through me, and I gulped. I'd apologize endlessly after it was all over if anyone gave me the chance.

"Why not?" I asked, forcing my hand to sit on my hip and wishing I knew what Em did with her feet to stand so confidently. "I'm the only Foretold here. No one else matters, so I'm going first." As I spoke, my vision constricted to just the space in front of me, everything else blurring to darkness in the edges. I strode past everyone into the testing room, unable to see their reactions even if I wanted to. Which I didn't.

As soon as I made it to the table with paper and pencils, I gripped the edge and leaned my weight against it. I squeezed my eyes shut while I breathed deeply, fighting to keep my inhalations slow. Ethyl was dead. Killed during a test, and they expected us to go on like nothing happened. I was ashamed that a lesser concern occurred to me while Ethyl's body lay in the next room—I had cemented my reputation as an Elite bitch in the eyes of every person in the foyer.

Heart fluttering, I tried to recall the feeling I'd taken away from the lightning bolts. My hands shook as I wrote the unfathomable number of deaths. Two hundred and three.

Over two *hundred* Seers would die in the next banning of their ability. Would it be like Kentucky, with skirmishes at the borders? Or would the next nation skip the hassle of jailing and round them up for execution? I still didn't understand the violent objection to such a helpful skill like Seerdom, so discerning how they would react was impossible without divination material. Unfortunately, all I had been allowed to predict was the end result. Two hundred and three.

I folded the paper and ran my fingers over the center crease four more times than was necessary. After leaving the testing room and delivering my paper to Granger, I looked only at Ethyl's body. "I'm sorry," I said, then mustered what little control I had left to bolt up the stairs.

I didn't stop moving until I was in Em's room, where I dropped face down on my borrowed bed and let the tears fall.

CHAPTER 20

Someone knocked.

I considered ignoring it, but after a brief silence, the knock came again.

And again.

I raised my head from the tear-soaked pillow. Daylight streamed through the crack in the curtains. Em was in bed, but it didn't look like the knocking had woken her.

Unable to find a tissue, I grabbed a sock out of my clothing box and used it to blow my nose. My sleeve took care of the tears.

Male voices conversed in easy tones in the hallway, too relaxed to be agents.

I opened the door and gasped in surprise. Deep-set blue eyes stared into mine, flicking rapidly to assess every nuance of my face. Dark bags underlined the eyes, and wrinkles fanned out from the sides. Why was Vance's dad here?

"There's our girl," he said, and opened his arms.

The invitation was too tempting. I stepped into the hallway and eased the door closed with my foot, hoping to let Em sleep in more. I didn't stop moving until the legendary comfort of a Peter Oleski hug engulfed me.

Fearing more tears, I stepped back sooner than I wanted to.

"Hi, Peter," I said, mustering a small smile.

"We missed you so much," he said.

"Dad." Vance's voice came from behind him, drawn out in warning.

Peter ignored it and beamed at me. "We *all* missed you."

"I missed you, too. All of you," I confessed.

"I came to pick up Vance for a visit to his mother. You know how she gets when the kids stay away too long." He winked conspiratorially at me. "I made Vance show me which room was yours, because I want you to come, too."

My chest squeezed in on itself. I'd abandoned them all. Aside from my letter to Vance, I hadn't said goodbye or thanks for the memories, or anything to anyone else. And here was Peter, with a sick wife and a pregnant daughter on bedrest, treating me like I was part of the family.

"I can't," I said, struggling to keep my breathing steady amid my swirling emotions.

"I told you," Vance said. "Let's go."

"Wait!" I called, then winced, hoping my yell hadn't woken Em through the thin walls. "I want to, so much. I actually can't." My gaze shifted from Peter to Vance. "It's always about what I'm allowed, not what I want."

Vance's eyes widened, and his lips parted with a small, sharp intake of breath. It was out there again—that I wanted to be with him, then and now, but he wouldn't acknowledge it any more than he did back then.

Peter stepped to the side, removing himself from the line of sight between Vance and me. After several quiet, stubborn moments, he sighed. "You're sure, then, Tallie?"

At my nod, he threw a loose arm over Vance's shoulders. He waved to me, his smile dimmer than it had been before, and they left, unaware that my heart stretched desperately after them.

I stayed in the hallway for a long time after they left, inspired by a substitute dad hug to wonder how my parents fared. It was strange, not knowing what city they were in, where they worked, what house they were in. Would they watch the broadcast of the competition? They might not. I didn't have any way of knowing their level of shame that their lone child had failed every one of their expectations. Watching me compete for a spot that should've already been mine would be too much. They probably didn't know I was part of the Oracus Test.

Maybe Em was awake. Being alone while missing my parents felt unwise. Her usual series of vague insults weren't much better, but they beat wallowing. At the very least, her presence guaranteed a distraction.

I reached for the doorknob but stopped at the sound of heavy footsteps in the hallway.

Two agents approached me, faces grim as ever. Hoping to avoid being manhandled, I walked toward them before they reached me.

"I'm coming," I said.

One man led the way downstairs, but the other hung back to follow me. Like I would try to run away from the director's agents with his last threat hanging over my head.

They led me outside to the silver car. Hooper occupied the backseat. As soon as I was buckled, the agents got in the front, and we drove.

"I trust you understand the future the test asked you to predict." The director leaned toward me by one purposeful, menacing inch.

"I understand it's horrible," I said with a shudder, not knowing what else there was to glean from the persecution of Seers. "And none of this is worth someone dying," I added in barely more than a whisper.

He sighed heavily, for too long, and shook his head. "You don't understand. Such a pity people blessed with insight into the future can't be wise in other ways."

"I'm sorry," I said in reflex. It was clear I should have picked up on some greater meaning behind the most recent test questions but had failed at that particular nuance.

"Things could always be worse. Imagine if someone with a strong Seer talent were to be exiled from a friendly nation and sent somewhere that has recently made such practices illegal."

I gasped, flinching away toward the door. "Why would anyone do that?"

Director Hooper laughed. The sound cut through the car without enough space to disperse its sharp edges. The harsh tones ricocheted and bounced around me as he wiped a nonexistent tear from under one eye.

"The naivety is more annoying than refreshing, you should know, but you respond so well to encouragement. I'm very much rooting for you to win this competition. I can't help observing how good you have it right now. How sad it would be to make a mistake, costing you all your current privileges."

Another threat. "Why do you want me to be a Seer so badly?" I asked, wishing my voice hadn't shaken so much.

"Show me how well you follow directions, and you won't have to worry about a thing," he said.

I didn't know how they timed the end of our drive at that exact moment, but the car pulled to a stop. The agent in the passenger seat got out and opened my door. He didn't give me a chance to respond to the director before he grabbed me by the upper arm and pulled me out of the car.

They drove off, leaving me bewildered and rubbing the ache where I'd been grabbed.

I was outside the dormitory. If I hurried, I could leave before the agent in the foyer noticed and grabbed me. But where would I go? My mind flashed to the Oleski's house, but I couldn't bring any government attention to them. They were dealing with enough already. My parents were … absent. I could stay with Carinne at the apprentice dormitory, but for how long? I faced exile to a nation that had banned divination, and that was on top of the original threat of losing things—*people*—that were important to me.

With a defeated shake of my head, I trudged back inside the building. There wasn't a point in resisting. It was what I wanted, too. Seerdom was my lifelong focus, the only thing that made me worthwhile. I'd abandoned the people who had meant the most to me to commit fully to my future.

I jerked to a stop in the foyer. My eyes trained on the spot where Ethyl's body had lain, smoking and lifeless.

Was the director this desperate for more Seers, or was it all some grand manipulation I didn't understand?

"Tallie? Tallie?" the voice repeated itself before I broke free from the daze.

"Are you okay?" Mink asked. He entered the foyer, holding Hudson's hand, and they walked up to me.

"Not really," I said, then cleared my throat. "What are you guys doing here?"

"Looking for Vance," Hudson said, wrinkling his nose as he stared at my face. "I hate spreading bad news, but you don't look so great."

"Vance left with his dad. And I don't feel so great."

"No one's in the living room if you want to talk." Mink placed his free hand on my arm.

I wanted to say yes.

The agent at his foyer post behind Mink and Hudson shook his head. I didn't need the reminder not to spill any secrets. Director Hooper had taken care of that two car rides ago.

I looked down, not sure what to say. I didn't want to alienate my old friends when they were trying to build a bridge.

"Is it Em?" Hudson asked. "I heard you're rooming with her. I hope she's not rubbing that thing with Vance in your face."

"Way to go, Hudson, you made her look even sicker," Mink scolded.

"What? Are we not supposed to know about her crush?"

That got my attention off the floor. "Vance told you?" I asked, gasping amid the words. "He couldn't even reply to my letter, but he told everyone else about it?" I stumbled toward a chair and flopped down hard.

Hudson and Mink stared at me, then each other, then back at me.

"I bet everyone had fun laughing about it, too." I groaned and buried my face in my hands. "This is so humiliating."

"Uh, Tallie?" Hudson started, sounding much less confident than usual. "You lost me somewhere around asking if Vance told us."

I peeked at them through the gaps between my fingers.

Mink nodded. "Yeah, what letter?" he asked.

I dropped my hands to my lap and gaped at them. "If you don't know about the letter, how did you know I had feelings for him?"

Hudson burst out laughing until Mink smacked him in the stomach with the back of his hand.

"We didn't *know*, but we knew," Hudson said, recovering his breath. "If you know what I mean."

Mink smiled gently with closed lips. "We just assumed. You guys were always together and there was … something different in the way you looked at each other. I used to bother Hudson about it and ask why he never looked at me that way." A playful spark lit his eyes, and his smile grew.

"We had a bet going," Hudson chimed in, earning himself an exasperated look from Mink. "It doesn't matter, we both lost," he finished in a grumble.

"Do I want to know what the bet was?" I asked. My hands itched to cover my face again.

"Oh, it was about who would kiss who first. If Vance would make the first move or if you would," Hudson said casually, like talking about Vance and me kissing didn't set off fireworks in my stomach and chest. "I thought it would be you, for the record."

"Well, you both lost. Big time."

"There's a reason *we* weren't Foretold," Mink said.

"Vance can't stand me," I whispered, hating how the truth sounded out in the open.

Hudson and Mink shared a heavy look, holding it for long enough that I started getting anxious.

Mink broke away from the silent exchange first. "After you disappeared, Vance changed. It was hard for a while."

Something existed in the spaces between his words. He was holding back details, and I didn't know if it was to spare my feelings or to protect Vance's secrets.

Flashes of the Vance I knew back then passed through my mind. His easy grin, and the way he could turn anything into an adventure. How he would give anyone a hand, but in a subtle way, not highlighting why they needed help in the first place. I always swore he could be friends with anybody. Given five minutes, he'd find common ground. And the way he didn't shy away from the love he had for his family astonished me. Most guys were too busy acting tough, but not Vance. He'd kiss his mom on the cheek and go in for a dad hug any time, in front of anyone. He was even affectionate toward all his big brothers and sisters. When I used to lose myself in an unforetold fantasy land, I would imagine the involved, loving dad he might be someday.

This new version, with the icy stares, the cold dismissals, and the actual anger … It was such a stark difference. I hoped he hadn't been this way for the entire three years since I'd seen him last. I hoped he hadn't been like that with his parents. It would have broken their hearts.

"Was he like he is now, toward me?" I asked. "All prickly and kind of mean?"

Mink's eyes turned down at the sides, softening in a show of pity.

Hudson wrinkled his nose at me again. "Vance? No way. He just lost his spark for a while, you know?"

I shook my head. "I *don't* know." I wished I knew. I wished I could go back in time and stop my parents from finding out about my secret friends. While I was at it, I wouldn't have written that letter, either.

"I don't think it's our story to tell," Mink cut in before Hudson could share any details.

A gust of fresh air blew in as the foyer door opened.

"You're telling stories?" Vance asked.

I spun around to face him, guilt suddenly pricking at my senses, like he'd caught me doing something forbidden.

"Nah, we were actually looking for you," Hudson said.

"I was with my mom." Vance shifted his eyes to me for one short, uneasy moment. "She made me promise to ask you to visit her again, Tallie." His mouth twisted to the side as he delivered the invitation, taking some of the welcome away from the words.

"I wish I could," I said, turning my head toward the agent, standing still at his post. I wondered what he made of all the personal drama he witnessed since being assigned as part of my spy detail.

The man shook his head at me, a warning to not reveal that Director Hooper's orders were keeping me confined to the competition dormitory.

Vance must have caught the movement because a second later, he was standing toe-to-toe with the agent. "Why are you telling her what to do?" he asked in a steely, quiet way that sent a quick shiver through my shoulders.

Mink edged closer to me and placed his arm across my back as Hudson moved next to Vance.

"Hey," Hudson said lightly. "Maybe we don't step up to the scary government agent. Right?"

Vance didn't even look at his friend. "There's something going on around here. Someone died last night, and they acted like it was nothing. And they're messing with Tallie. I don't know what the hell they're doing, but I don't trust it."

"Someone died?" Mink whispered close to my ear.

I nodded, tears forming as he squeezed me in closer to his side like the last three years of separation had never happened. I wiped my eyes clear in time to see the agent brush aside his suit jacket and reach for something hooked at his waist.

"Vance!" I shouted. "I'm fine. I, um, I've been petitioning Director Hooper to name me the winner and put me in the Oracus right away. It's supposed to be a secret." The lies burned their way out of my mouth, leaving an aftertaste I couldn't get rid of fast enough. But I couldn't stand there and let Vance get into trouble or hurt—or worse—because Ethyl's death had triggered the protective instinct in him. He needed to back down. I needed him safe.

"Unbelievable," came a new voice from the kitchen door.

I looked over to see two of the remaining competitors, Kinsley and Maddoc, glaring at me.

"Completely believable," Maddoc said. "I knew she couldn't be trusted."

"If she'd followed through with teaching us her Seer crap, maybe Ethyl would've known how to stay safe in the storm. Maybe she wouldn't have died." Kinsley gestured to the spot on the floor where Vance had laid Ethyl's body down. Where he and Julion tried and failed to resuscitate her.

It wasn't their fault. That honor belonged to me. If I had taught the others about astrapomancy, I could've coached them on how to read it fast and when to ditch the storm for safety.

"You've got blood on your hands, bitch," Kinsley spat out.

Mink tried tightening his hold on me, fingers digging in with a protective grip, but I shoved myself free.

"I'm sorry. I'm so sorry," I said, and ran for the stairs, tears flowing down my face.

Maybe I *should* have petitioned Director Hooper for the chance to win the competition early like I had told Vance I was doing. They knew I had Seer talent already. He wanted me in place, fulfilling the prediction of the Seer who named me as a Foretold. I could spare the others from dangerous trials.

It would mean keeping secrets for the rest of my life. I'd been working so hard toward my Seerdom I never considered what it would truly be like, with the success and failure of Michigan riding on my skills. Compared to a Seer in the Oracus, I barely had any secrets to keep and I was already breaking down. If I became a Seer and messed something up, it would go beyond disappointing my parents. I'd fail the entire nation.

The thought alone pushed down on my shoulders, weighing me to the point I couldn't run anymore. I didn't make it to Em's room. I knelt under the pressure, then sat, scooting to press my back against the wall as hard as I could, needing to feel something solid. Black spots floated in to crowd my vision and my breathing quickened, inhaling more but getting less air. I gasped with each breath, desperate for oxygen, but not doing anything correctly to get it. I was simultaneously whirling away in space and being pressed down under the earth.

Nothing existed but a narrow patch of carpet in front of me. I rocked back and forth, squeezing my knees to my chest, barely noticing that my head hit the wall with each backward movement. One side of my body grew warm, but I couldn't care to find out why. I was dying. I deserved to die. Ethyl was my fault. So many people's lives and deaths could be my fault if I ascended into Seerdom with the Oracus. I couldn't handle it, but I wasn't anything without it. I was nothing after the failed entrance ceremony. Every day since proved that I didn't deserve my Foretelling.

I gasped in more air to sob, my body shaking with the anguished cry, but was unable to produce sound. A faint noise grew in the background. It remained close to nothing for a long time before the sounds and words took shape in my ears.

"I'm here. You're safe. I'm here. You're safe."

By the time I processed what the words meant, I realized it was Vance. He was the heat at my side and the voice that broke through my thoughts. I couldn't reply. My breathing came quicker.

"Breathe slower. Breathe slower. Shit. Tallie, feel me. Feel my breath. Match my breaths."

One of my hands was gently pried from its grip on my knee. It was drawn to the right, and I felt my palm pressing against the solid plane of Vance's chest.

"Match … my … breaths. Match … my … breaths." He spaced the words out, so they came in time with the rise and fall of his chest. "Match … my … breaths. Match … my … breaths."

He kept up the mantra, maintaining a slow steady pace with his breathing, though I could feel the frantic beating of his heart underneath it all. After an untold stretch of time, I felt every other one of my inhalations line up with his. I tried to absorb the simple repetition of his words and focus on the movement of his chest where he pressed my hand to his skin. The skin *under* his shirt, I realized, as I came back to the present.

Shaking, I aligned my breathing with his. He didn't stop the words, and he didn't let go of my hand. We sat together, pressed against the wall of the hallway, with my hand splayed across his chest. He guided our breathing until I stopped rocking, then stopped crying. I laid my head on his shoulder, too exhausted to hold it up anymore. The smell of his soap kept my focus on his presence, something real and solid and safe. He let go of my hand, and it slid down to his stomach, but I didn't have the power to move my hand out from underneath his shirt. He didn't move away, but continued his words faintly, diminishing to a breath of a whisper.

"Match my breaths. Match my breaths."

There, in the hallway, I fell asleep.

CHAPTER 21

"Not where I expected this to happen, but okay."

I blinked my eyes open to see Em smirking down at me.

"News is about to start," she said. "We're all supposed to be in the living room."

Vance was sitting beside me, propped against the wall. His arm and shoulder served as my pillow, and his shirt blanketed my hand, splayed across his abdomen. I sat up, horrified that I had trapped him by passing out after a panic attack, especially after he had been with his sick mom.

"I'm sorry," I said, leaning away to give him a chance to escape. He didn't.

"Tallie," he said, lilting his way across my name and sending a deep ache through my chest. "You don't have anything to apologize for."

That wasn't what he'd said the last time we discussed my apologies.

"Wow," Em said, her tone flat and dry. "You two have so much to unpack. But the creepy guys in suits said to get you both down there. Now."

"Tallie shouldn't have to go," Vance said as he got to his feet, then reached down to help me up.

Em shrugged. "Take that up with them. See you down there." She sauntered away to the stairs.

"You should go lay down," Vance insisted.

I lifted my chin and pushed my shoulders back, trying to project an air of stability. What a joke that was. "I'll be okay. Let's go."

It was the second lie I'd told him that day. I wouldn't be okay, not if we were on our way to hear about hundreds of Seers dying. Not if Ethyl's death was my fault. Not if my destiny as a Seer put the weight of a nation pressing down on me.

A muscle twitched in Vance's jaw, drawing my eye to the sharp line.

"I really did want to visit your mom," I said. "I always loved your family."

His lips pressed together, but the sides turned up in a semblance of a smile. "They are pretty lovable."

He'd been the most lovable of them all, but I wouldn't tell him. Not again, anyway.

"Any chance you'll tell me what's going on with the security detail?" he asked.

"Another thing I wish I could do, but it's not allowed. I'm sorry."

The edges of his eyes and the planes of his face softened, finally, familiarly, and he tipped forward. It was a motion I had seen him make countless times, when he would brush a whisper of a kiss on my forehead, right at my hairline. It had started after a couple months of hanging out, when we would say goodbye for the day. I closed my eyes, but the brief touch of his lips never came. I heard a sigh and opened my eyes again, cheeks burning in fear that he knew what I'd incorrectly assumed.

Vance retreated several steps backward and clenched his arms across his chest. The tight, small smile was back and the tension in his eyes suggested he was hiding a different emotion. "Let's go before those goons come looking for us."

I nodded and dragged my weary body downstairs to the living room.

The others had all claimed seats. Two spots on a couch were open between the arm and where Em sat. Not wanting to look insecure, I hurried forward to claim the spot next to the arm, leaving the space next to Em open for Vance.

Granger and two agents stood in front of the room, eyeing the small group of contestants. There should have been one more person in the room. Was everyone else thinking of Ethyl, too? I glanced around, trying to read their faces, and jerked my head in a double take. Hudson and Mink huddled together in the oversized chair;

Pedestrians mixed in with Oracus hopefuls. Hudson's face was almost unrecognizable in its anger. Mink wore an expression of concern. Maybe fear, though I had never seen it on him before, so it was hard to tell.

The static of the radio announced the beginning of the news.

"Missibama, attempting to avoid the riots and unrest of its Seer-banning predecessors, gathered a group of two hundred and twenty practicing Seers prior to announcing their new law."

"Yes," Julion whispered. "I got it right."

"Seventeen of those Seers pledged to renounce their newly illegal practices. Two hundred and three were executed by congressional order."

I dropped my head until my chin rested on my chest. Any remaining energy after the panic attack drained right out of me. *Executed.* I didn't understand why Seerdom was becoming illegal in the first place, so there was no way I could fathom having them killed for their talent.

"Julion, Marie, and Hannah, you have been eliminated from the competition," Granger said. "If you could collect your belongings, you will be escorted from the building."

An agent stepped forward and held out a hand to quiet Granger. "No one will be leaving, by order of Director Hooper."

Gasps and exclamations rang through the room, but Hudson and Mink didn't join in the surprised reactions. Vance's body tensed next to me, and I had to stop myself from reaching for his hand. His comfort wasn't mine to claim.

The agent continued, "News of the contestant's death will be contained until after the competition is over. Anyone with knowledge of the incident is confined to this house for the remainder of the test."

"To ensure your continued safety," the other agent added after a moment's pause.

His voice pricked at my memory. They all looked so similar, but he could have been the man who drove me to the apprentice dormitory. For him to break the customary silence of agents, to offer minor comforts, I hoped he wouldn't get in trouble. He seemed almost human.

Voices filtered into the living room from the direction of the foyer:

"Don't rush her," a man insisted. "She's not well."

"I'm fine. It's Liann they need to look out for."

I knew those voices.

Vance shot to his feet and bolted down the hallway. Concern replenished enough of my energy to follow at a slower pace.

Peter and Gina stood in the foyer, side by side. Peter held two overnight bags in one hand, and his other arm wrapped around Gina's waist. Her face held the same drawn appearance it had when I saw her through the window at her home. Her clothes hung off her frame, baggier than she usually wore, and she sagged against Peter. A seated Liann emerged through the door, her face red and scowling, with an agent pushing her wheelchair into the center of the foyer.

"What's going on?" Vance asked, rushing to his mom's open side.

"Oh, sweetie!" his mother exclaimed, only then noticing him. "We're getting moved here for a week or two. Something about security."

"Something like bullshit," Liann groused under her breath.

"After I dropped you off here, one of these goons followed me home and informed us we would be moving immediately," Peter ground out the words, glaring at the man behind Liann's wheelchair.

Director Hooper had dropped me off shortly before Vance got back to the dormitory from visiting his parents. They could have seen Vance's dad and assumed he had learned about Ethyl.

The directorate forcefully moved a cancer patient and a pregnant girl who wasn't supposed to leave her bed. It was the Oleskis. They were the best people I had ever met, and if Hooper had explained the seriousness of the situation, they would've kept the knowledge to themselves. There wasn't any reason to upend their lives. Maybe Vance hadn't even *told* them what happened to Ethyl.

All questions and explanations were cut short as the agents steered the newcomers down a lesser-used hallway at the back of the foyer. Vance stayed on their heels and glowered at the man pushing Liann's wheelchair until he ceded control of it. The agent followed them, as if the—the *prisoners* would make a run for it.

The air stirred and warmed behind me. I turned to see Hudson and Mink flanking my sides.

"One of them heard us talking about Ethyl in front of you," I said, guessing why they were still here.

"Yeah, we're not allowed to leave," Hudson said. "Apparently, we're excused from our apprenticeships for a week, so that part's not bad, but I don't trust this."

Mink shook his head. "Me either."

I sighed in resigned agreement.

"Gina looks worse," Hudson said, worrying his mouth to one side.

I agreed again. How many days had it been since I saw her? Not enough to have her looking so … small.

"Vance says she has good days and bad days," Mink said. "Maybe this is a bad day."

My heart clenched painfully. Vance had to win the competition. Gina needed treatment, not an endless wait for medical care to become available, using time she didn't have. Could I help Vance win without Director Hooper catching me? Could I tamper with the future in a way that might not be compatible with existing predictions? For in the Oracus, there could be a Seer who already knew how this competition would end.

CHAPTER 22

I waited until Vance left the wing of the building that housed his parents and sister. He rushed to the stairs, not looking up at anyone. My heart begged to go after him, but I needed to see his family. I didn't know much about cancer. No one I knew had ever been that sick, so I didn't know if Gina would live or die. I couldn't let her leave this world without her knowing what her involvement in my life had meant; how special she was.

I walked down the hall, hoping I wasn't making a huge mistake by intruding on their personal struggles. It could be all awkward silences and hints that I should leave. My feet kept going, though, powered by some hidden confidence that rarely took control.

I reached a door at the end of the hallway, knocked three times, then waited.

Peter opened the door with tense shoulders and his chest puffed up with a deep breath, ready to argue *something*. At the sight of me, his shoulders relaxed, and he let the breath go in one long swoop. "Tallie, come in," he said.

I entered behind him and found myself in an actual home within the dormitory. We stood in a small living room with an attached kitchen. No dining area. Three doors led out from the living space. Two were open, revealing a bedroom and a bathroom. Gina sat in the living room, but Liann was nowhere to be seen. I bet the third door was her bedroom.

Gina's weary face lit up and rose around the sagging edges when I walked in.

"Tallie, dear, come here!" She reached her arms toward me. I rushed to the couch, and she wrapped me in a hug as soon as my butt hit the cushion.

"I'm so sorry. I didn't know you were sick," I said, pulling back to let her see my earnest expression.

"Psh," she said. "I don't typically bring it up. It ruins appetites. I suppose it's a little more obvious on days like this, though."

"Can I do anything to help?" I asked, blushing at the inadequacy of my offer. Nothing I knew how to do would be helpful. The Seerdom I aimed toward, most of my life's accomplishments and points of pride; they were totally useless when it came to this. My mind flashed to Ethyl's still and smoking body. I was useless when it came to a lot of things.

"You're doing it right now," Peter said as he sat in a chair across the small room from Gina and me. "Just visit when you can. Distractions are good."

"I'm sorry they moved you here, but it's so good to see you. I, uh," I stammered and ducked my head, hoping to hide my blush, "really, really missed you guys."

Gina nodded, a small, closed smile playing across her mouth.

I took a deep breath. "Hopefully this is okay, but I want you to know how much you all meant to me before I stopped coming around … back then."

"It's okay," Peter started.

Gina cut him off with a loud shush. "She's not done talking, dear."

"Sorry," I said.

Both of Vance's parents waved off the word.

"My parents are great and everything, but sometimes, or all the time, my house had so much pressure in it. Everything was about my future as a Seer. It was behind everything we did and talked about. Then I met Vance and his friends, and for the first time since I was little, I was allowed to be a person, not just a future Seer. I wasn't supposed to hang around, um, Pedestrians," I stumbled over the word in front of Peter and Gina, "so I told my parents I was studying or practicing with other Foretolds. Then I met your family. Everyone could be themselves—appreciated and loved for who they already were, not who they could be or what they could become."

"That'd be Gina's influence," Peter said with a sly smile before Gina shushed him again. She patted the top of my leg, prompting me to keep going.

"So, I started showing up more and more, and my parents noticed. They found out where I was going and who I was spending time with, and they thought I was going to abandon my goals. Or, you know, their goals. They said I couldn't go back. They told me everything being Foretold had done for our family, and what would happen if I didn't become a Seer, and it sounded so scary, and …" I trailed off, the inside of my throat becoming too thick.

Peter rose from his chair and sat on the couch on my other side. Gina put a thin arm around my lower back and Peter draped his heavier arm across my shoulders.

I gathered my voice and carried on with my confession, "They'll only love me if I become a Seer," I whispered. "So, I stopped coming around. I left my best friends and the best family I'd ever met. The only goodbye I said was in a letter to Vance. I, um, I'm sorry, this might be weird to say to you, but I loved him. And I told him in the letter and offered to sneak out and see him, but he never met me. He never replied, and I dove into my Seerdom and that was it until the ceremony." That was all I could say on that front.

The Oleskis were already aware of more than the director wanted them to be. I wouldn't dig them in deeper with knowledge of my Foretelling being mistaken.

I took a breath to refocus my thoughts. "But I never forgot you. I only knew you guys for a year, but it was the happiest I've ever been. The most I ever felt like me, and that gave me something to hold on to when the pressure of being Foretold got to be too much. So, this was a really long way to say thank you. Thank you so much for accepting me as Tallie the kid, instead of Natalie the prodigy Foretold."

"Oh, sweetheart," Gina started, but a loud, triumphant laugh from the second bedroom interrupted.

"I *told* you she had it bad for him!" Liann's voice carried from behind the closed door, but wood and distance didn't muffle the smugness of her tone a bit.

Peter sighed. "Probably not helpful right now, sweetie," he called back.

My face burned with a tenacious blush.

Gina squeezed my side. "Don't be embarrassed," she said. "I think Vance is pretty lovable myself. I always thought your disappearance had something to do with being Foretold. A couple of the boys thought you used them for some rebellion or other before remembering you were an Elite, and 'too good for them.' I never bought that for a second, but I did always wonder about the truth."

We sat in silence for a few moments before Peter cleared his throat.

"I never heard anything about a letter," he said slowly, haltingly, like the words might trip a landmine.

"Me either," Gina said. "Vance took you leaving hard."

"Why?" I asked. "He could have met me or gotten in touch with me or something. Anything. But he left me hanging." It had been three years, and the ache of mystery never left.

"We don't know," Gina said. "He never would talk about you."

"I'm sorry," I said. "I didn't mean to pry. I really did just mean to thank you and explain why you all meant so much to me."

"We understand," Peter said.

Gina bobbed her head up and down in agreement. "What have your parents said since the ceremony?" she asked.

"I don't know," I said, staring at my knees.

"What do you mean?" she asked.

"They haven't reached out since being moved. Maybe they're not allowed to. We never got to say goodbye, or talk about how I ruined our futures, or anything." I shrugged. "I might never know, and it might be for the best. They must be relieved to be rid of such a disappointment."

Gina inhaled sharply, causing Peter to tense up. Then she shook her head. "You might not understand this until you're a mother someday yourself, but the capacity for loving our children is big. Huge. More than sense, pride, or anything else. I wouldn't write them off quite yet."

Tears welled in my eyes as I accepted the hug they sandwiched me in. When they released me, I stood from the couch and wiped my eyes. "I better go," I said weakly. "But, um, can I come back tomorrow?"

Gina scoffed. "You better!" she said. "I'll take it as a personal insult if you don't chat with me every chance you get."

Laughing the tears away, I left their room and returned to the foyer. A chill ran down my spine when I came into sight of the agent standing guard. He stared at me with a level of suspicion and menace that had me staggering back a step. I froze, waiting for him to grab me and drag me off to another private meeting with the director, but he made no movements.

Forcing steel into my shoulders, I skirted around the other side of the room to the stairs. I bolted up, unable to shake the feeling of being chased, though the agent remained down in the foyer.

Curiosity over Vance's silence toward me still burned within. His mom said he took it hard after I stopped coming around, and that didn't fit within my assumptions at all. I could puzzle over that for eternity, ramp up my anxiety, and be miserable with constant curiosity. Or I could summon my courage and ask him why.

I marched down the hallway, intent on my choice. I stopped at the end of the hall, right in the middle between Vance's room and Em's room. Turning to the left, I knocked.

Julion answered the door, face stuck in a sullen funk.

"Hey," I said, suddenly shy. "Is Vance here?"

Julion shook his head. "Try across the hall. He went over there like twenty minutes ago."

He was in Em's room? If he'd been looking for me, he wouldn't have stayed there for twenty minutes. But I was set on finding out the answers, ready to pull myself from the infinite *why*. It wasn't like I'd be barging in somewhere private—it was kind of my room. Em had invited me, and my stuff was there. I had every right to go in, or so I told myself. Whether I believed my justifications was beside the point.

In a slight daze, I turned from Julion without remembering to thank him and walked across the hall. I opened the door to Em's room and froze.

Vance sat on Em's bed. She was kneeling on the bed, leaning into him, their arms wrapped around each other.

My heart, coated in flames, plummeted to the earth, scorching everything inside me on its way down. I turned and ran. Ran down the hall, down the stairs, then realized I had nowhere to go. Nowhere to hide, even if I was allowed to leave—which I wasn't. I had no one, nowhere, nothing. I couldn't go back upstairs, I couldn't stay in the foyer with the agent watching me, I couldn't go back to Vance's parents. They'd notice in a second how I was struggling to hold back tears and heartbreak. Shoulders slumped in defeat, I decided on the living room, which was empty thanks to our dwindling numbers.

I had no right to be so broken up over seeing them together. Vance hadn't returned my feelings three years ago. He hadn't said anything to contradict that since we came back into each other's lives. I *knew* he'd been involved with Em, despite the news that they had broken things off. People changed their minds all the time.

My eyes flicked to the pile of sticks tucked at the edge of the room. There was no need to drift in uncertainty when I wasn't entirely without skills. Performing predictions as a normal citizen, not a Foretold or a Seer, was against the law in every nation. But I *had* been Foretold, and I was almost a Seer. It was close enough to be permissible, and I was trapped in the competition dormitory for now, anyway. Who could I possibly reveal sensitive information to? A scary man in a gray suit?

After running my sleeve over my eyes and sniffing in hard, I gathered the sticks into my arms. What could I predict that wouldn't break my heart further? Not Vance's future—it would most certainly showcase his life without me in it. Seeking one's own future was taboo. It was fine to predict things that were involved in my life, but purely self-driven questions were frowned upon. I couldn't discern who would win the competition. If it wasn't Vance, I wouldn't be able to look Gina in the eyes, knowing she had to fight her cancer without treatment.

My parents. I could look for their general situation in the future. I could know for certain they were safe; they had to be. I could picture where they lived, form an image of them doing their various daily tasks, anytime I felt homesick.

I formed the question: *Where will my parents be in one week?* Everything else faded away, save for a lingering Vance-related nausea I hoped wouldn't stay with me always. I tapped my fingers against the bundle of sticks, familiarizing myself with them. Projecting the question into them, I closed my eyes and cast the sticks before me. They pattered softly onto the carpet, and I opened my eyes.

My attention snagged on a chaotic heap, loosely framed by other sticks in non-parallel lines. I couldn't look away. My breathing grew ragged, harder to draw in oxygen, but so very different from a panic attack. It was like a large set of jaws clamped around my chest and compressed, forcing me to fight for every molecule of oxygen.

All I could envision was water. Deep, chilled, and lapping against a lightly pebbled, sandy shore.

My parents were underneath.

CHAPTER 23

"Young lady. *Young lady*," a voice repeated, jarring me from the prediction.

Blinking rapidly, it was difficult to orient myself back to the present. Granger stood before me with red cheeks, hands on his hips, and eyebrows raised.

I cleared my throat, opened my mouth, and nothing came out. After another heavy throat clearing, I croaked out an apology for making him wait.

"What do you think you're doing?" Granger asked. "Is this an attempt at subverting the competition process?"

One of the agents stood behind him, arms crossed in a way that made his muscles bulge bigger than normal.

I shook my head to answer and clear the cobwebs of divination from my mind.

"I wanted to know where my parents live. When I'm missing them, I'd like to think of them properly—where they are, instead of where they used to be."

A rapid clicking started directly after my shaky words. It took a moment to realize my teeth were chattering. My whole body shivered, and I wrapped my arms around myself in an ineffective grasp at warmth. I could shake my head and blink my eyes a million times, and it still wouldn't erase the lingering feeling that my parents faced a watery grave. In a week, if not sooner.

It couldn't be true. They had moved. I did everything Director Hooper demanded of me, so he had no reason to kill them. Ethyl died because I followed his instructions to keep my parents safe. They couldn't die. People had to stop *dying*.

Divination with sticks was my least favorite, the least reliable method. I was reeling from seeing Vance with Em, feeling guilty about Ethyl's death, and worrying about Gina. My head wasn't in the right place to get an accurate prediction. That was it. It had to be.

"We can't have you divining anything outside of competition events," Granger said, glancing from me to the agent, then back to me. "This process isn't a game or a lark. It is for the betterment and security of our nation. It will be treated as such." He drew himself up while speaking. By the time he finished, his shoulders were thrown back, his chest puffed out, and he jutted his chin forward.

Half of me wanted to apologize and half wanted to salute with sarcasm. All I did was nod. I was relieved of any responsibility to respond further when the four other remaining contestants entered the room. Vance was trying his hardest to catch my eye. I clung harder to my composure.

The others found seats, all able to claim separate pieces of furniture. I chewed on my lower lip and tried to keep my eyes on Granger.

"Would you like to be seated?" he asked me, after an extended group silence.

I shook my head and kept hugging myself. My teeth had stopped chattering, but stray bouts of shivering still coursed through me.

"Okay," he said, drawing out the word, then turned to the other four contestants. "Your next test is in the morning due to the difficulty of divining after a disturbing event. You may take the remainder of the day and night to rest. We would like the most accurate result, ensuring we will receive the best candidates to support our nation. Gather here at nine am. Miss Kowalczyk has graciously provided the wood needed for the event."

My divination sticks. Granger bent to gather them and dumped them into the brick fireplace that decorated the long front wall of the room.

There went my only material for an assisted divination. Tomorrow's test would undoubtedly be flames. I didn't think I could gather anything else without being noticed breaking the new rule. No predicting the future outside of what the competition required. I wouldn't have the chance to confirm or refute my parents' future. I bet I couldn't sneak back into the living room once everyone was gone and retrieve the sticks without Mr. Biceps in the suit catching me.

Another question with no available answer: Was it a faulty reading or would my parents die?

If I lost the competition, I would have no one. Despite the pressure my parents put on me, they also gave me as good of a life as they could. I was never neglected or abused or made to feel unwanted. They were home. They were all I had known, aside from school with the Foretolds and my year of stolen joy with Vance and his crew. The other Foretolds, including Bryla, hadn't paused during the entrance ceremony to check on me or offer any sympathetic words. They'd marched past my humiliation, unwilling to look straight at me. If I didn't join them in the Oracus, I wouldn't be anything to them. In a week or less, my parents wouldn't be anything at all, aside from dead, and I didn't know how to stop it.

I lost control of the shivering as my focus turned to holding back tears.

"Tallie, can I talk to you?" Vance asked.

A dagger to my heart, his voice lanced me open.

"You don't have to," I said. "I understand why you didn't want me staying in Em's room."

Vance's eyes widened, eyebrows raised and drawn together. His mouth parted in a small O. In a rush, he said, "Please, come up to my room. I'll get Julion to leave. I think we left a lot of things unsaid between us."

"One of us did," I mumbled.

"What?" He leaned in closer like he could catch my words after the fact.

I shook my head. Even if he was back with Em, I could finally learn what he thought three years ago after he read my letter. My heart was broken either way. It had been all along but seeing him in this competition had reopened the wound. It would be better if I knew exactly how unwelcome my feelings were. I could move on with that level of closure.

Still staring at me with that hesitant, wide-open gaze, he waited for an answer.

I left the living room, nerves increasing with each sound of his steps behind me. When we reached the foyer, Hudson and Mink emerged from the kitchen.

Hudson's face lit up. "Hey, look at you two—"

Mink clapped a hand over Hudson's mouth, staring at him intently, then slowly eased his hand away.

"Look at you two … stuck inside in *this* kind of weather," Hudson said, backtracking his words and staring out the window at the gray sky and steady rain.

Beside him, Mink dropped his chin and sighed, shaking his head.

Vance stayed as close to me as possible until we reached his room. He entered first and groaned loudly.

Em was sitting on one of the beds, chatting with Julion across the room. She interrupted their conversation when she saw me. "Tallie, I need—"

Vance stopped her. "I'll tell her everything. Can you guys get out of here for a while?"

Of all the extra senses, telling the future was proving more and more worthless. There was nothing I could do but stand silent, wishing I could turn invisible to hide my burning shame, as Em and Julion shuffled out of the room. I backed up to a side wall and didn't look up until the door shut.

Vance and I were alone.

CHAPTER 24

He ran a hand through his hair and blew out a long breath. Under my stare, he chuckled, just for a second, and glanced around the room, never settling on any particular point for long.

I had waited three years, wondering. That was enough. There was too much else going wrong to stay tortured and distracted over an unrequited crush.

"Why didn't you meet me?" I asked. "You could have written back and told me you didn't feel the same, but you left it *all* unsaid. Was I that insignificant?"

Vance pressed his lips together, hard enough that when he released them, they stayed white for a few seconds before regaining their color. "I didn't know about the letter."

My eyes narrowed. "What do you mean? I left it in your mailbox myself."

"I never got the letter, Tallie."

He needed to stop saying my name like that. It would only make this harder to hear. Couldn't he just rush through the sounds, rendering them inconsequential like everyone else?

"One day, you stopped coming by," he said. "You'd been there every day, and I guess I forgot you were Foretold. It seemed like you'd be there always, and then you were gone."

"I wasn't just gone, I—" I'd explained *everything* in that letter. Why hadn't he gotten it?

"Your parents came to my house."

I gaped at him, not caring how it looked. How did they know where he lived?

"They told me you got all your rebellion out of your system, and that I shouldn't try contacting you, in case my bad influence *infected* you again. They said you realized you couldn't risk your future by," he swallowed, "associating with degenerates that could only drag you down."

The betrayal sunk deep. I didn't question that story for a moment. My parents were always concerned about my focus on my path as Foretold. After our rise to Elite status, they snubbed everyone we had known before as Pedestrians.

"Why are you telling me this now?"

He explained why he never answered my letter, why he never kept in contact, but nothing hinted in the slightest that he'd wanted anything aside from friendship. The one bright spot, amidst all the dreary and dim, was that he never read my confession of feelings. My humiliation on that front could subside. He'd learn from this conversation that I had a crush on him, but the details and the depth … those would stay safely inside me.

"After I saw my parents today," he said, "I went back to my room to deal with things on my own. But I realized pretty quickly I wanted to share it with you. Even if you thought you were too good for me, for our friends, you've always loved my parents. It seemed right to let you know what's happening with Mom. I looked in your room first, but only Em was there."

I grabbed for a lock of my hair and ran my fingers through it, over and over, needing something to ground me to reality.

"She looked into your past, Tallie. Julion told her some things about the way you left us, and she didn't quite buy it. She did her own research."

My fingers stilled, clutching the strands of hair like a lifeline as I waited for what Em had seen, what she had revealed to him.

"Your parents made you stop coming. You put a letter in my mailbox. You waited, halfway between our houses, freezing outside until the middle of the night." His voice roughened, and he paused to clear his throat. "Em didn't see what was in that letter, Tallie, but she saw you in the days after you left it."

He took a step toward me.

Mirroring his actions, I moved one step forward as well, grip still firm on the ends of my hair.

"She had to look farther back in your past, then check those days again, because she thought someone important in your life had died. That's how torn up you looked."

I shook my head. "No one died, aside from who I wished I could be."

"Who did you wish you could be?" he asked quietly, taking one more step forward.

I followed his lead and closed the gap between us by one more step.

"I wanted to be someone you could love." I didn't look away or hide as I made my confession, finally finding the bravery that had been missing since the day I left that letter.

Vance cleared the final distance between us. He stood a breath away from me, staring down with those deep-set blue eyes that I never stopped dreaming about. He reached for the hand that clutched my hair and eased my grip. My hand fell to my side, and his replaced it, gently stroking a finger through the length of my hair before brushing it behind me. The side of his hand grazed my shoulder on the way, and I sucked in a sharp intake of air.

"Tallie," he said, taking his time with my name, hypnotizing me with how he shaped his mouth and tongue around it, more sigh than sound. "That's who you've always been."

I rose onto my toes, wanting to breathe in the air that carried those beautiful words. He dipped his chin and pressed his lips to mine in a soft, unhurried glance of a kiss that was over as soon as it registered in my senses. His hands cupped my shoulders, then he took his time trailing his fingertips down my arms.

Moving was out of the question. I was afraid if I did, the moment would vanish, and reality would barge back in. But his lips stayed near mine with the barest distance between them. He was waiting for me to answer his timid question of a kiss with one of my own.

With shaking fingers, I laid my palms flat against his chest, over his collarbone. He stayed impossibly still. I slid my hands up behind his neck and reached my fingertips into his auburn hair. Anchored exactly where I needed to be, I tipped my chin up and our lips met again. He sighed against me, and his hands ceased their fragile exploration. They twined around my back and pulled me into him.

He kissed me with such care and depth that I didn't care if I did anything else for the rest of my life.

I didn't hear the door open.

"Ugh, finally," Em said, her dry voice breaking into my elation. "You guys were killing the rest of us with the tension."

Our kiss ended. I tried to step away from Vance, not sure how to be polite about making out in front of someone he used to be involved with. Vance's arms didn't budge, though. He didn't turn to the door, didn't take his gaze from me for a second, as if he hadn't noticed the interruption.

"If I had known how you felt, Tallie," he whispered, trailing off as his eyes dipped to my lips and stayed there for a heavy, silent moment. "I don't need to see the future to know that no one will ever live up to you. It's always been you, but I never wanted to get in the way of your goals."

A blazing thrill shot through me before dousing itself in cold water. Em was in the room. Vance's words were everything I wanted to hear, but did he have to say them in front of her?

I looked behind him, but Em was gone. Julion was nowhere to be seen either, and the door was closed. I cringed and looked back at Vance. My stomach lurched with guilt; not only for Em, but for kissing Vance and hashing out our feelings when my parents could be in danger.

"I think we scared Em away," I said, unable to voice the larger worry in my mind.

"That's who came in here?" Vance closed his eyes for longer than a blink should have lasted.

I couldn't imagine myself being enchanting enough that he didn't recognize her voice.

"Did you see us hugging earlier?" he asked.

I nodded and started finger-combing my hair again. There was still that uncomfortable scene to work out. I didn't think Vance was a player, but the last three years of his life were a mystery to me.

"I asked her for help, now that I know she can see the past. My parents won't say much about my mom's cancer. It was driving me crazy. I asked Em to look into my mom's past, to when she was diagnosed."

Thinking back to the scene I had broken in on earlier, I pictured Vance's defeated slump as he sat on the edge of Em's bed. Her arms had been around his shoulders, face turned away from his. If I hadn't been so raw, so vulnerable, I would've seen it for what it was—comfort. His mom's diagnosis was bad.

"They think she has six months to live."

My eyes welled up, and through my blurred sight, I saw Vance wipe away tears of his own.

"But if you win this, would Elite medical care change that?" I hoped, I hoped.

He shook his head. "She could have had the best treatment possible from the day of her diagnosis, and it wouldn't have made a difference. Tallie, she's going to die."

My tears fell then, and I pulled Vance into a crushing hug that he returned with equal force. We clung together, mourning the future of his mother—the heart of his family, the irreplaceable woman who had shown me what love and acceptance truly meant. We didn't need to talk. I didn't feel the need to apologize. All I could do was be there, be present with him.

Our grief over his mom's future opened my mind to the prediction about my parents coming true. It wasn't the time to bring it up, to take away from this moment for Gina. I didn't let go of Vance until his grip on me slackened. He glanced at the door.

"Do you want to see what they needed?" I asked, thinking of Em and Julion's earlier interruption.

"No," Vance said simply.

We shared a short, tearful laugh.

"Do you?" he asked.

"No." I wiped my eyes and smiled up at him, broken-hearted over his mother, but deeply grateful I'd be with him, with *them*, for the rest of this journey. "But we probably should."

Vance sighed and found my hand with his, lacing our fingers together like they were a matching set.

This feeling was the only thing I ever wanted that someone else didn't choose for me. I thought it was beyond my reach, but it finally came … when nothing else was as it should've been.

Keeping our hands entwined, Vance drew our arms up and looped his over my head, so he could have his arm around me and hold my hand at the same time. My heart skipped and pranced, temporarily distracted from the mire it had been stuck in. Tucked close together, we left his room and crossed the hall. I reached for the knob, then hesitated. He had *been* with Em here.

Vance tilted his head to look down at me, puzzling over my pause. I pulled my hand out of his grasp and ducked out from under his arm. How could I ask about it without humiliating myself? My cheeks burned as I considered just stuffing my doubts deep down and acting like they weren't there.

"I thought you hated me," I said, breaking the silence with a truth, though it wasn't the truth currently weighing me down.

His face crumpled; fine lines splaying out from the wince in his eyes and his freckles standing out more than usual. "I hated being hurt," he said. "How I couldn't get over you, even though I wasn't good enough for you. Seeing you and knowing we couldn't pick up where we left off. Was I being a complete asshole?"

I nodded, smiling slightly to soften the news.

"I'm sorry," he said, leaning forward to kiss my temple. He gestured to the door. "And about this; even before I thought you and I had a chance, I told Em that we couldn't … spend any time together anymore."

"I wish you hadn't told me about your feelings in front of her."

He tilted his head to the side, trying to get a better line of sight into my eyes. "Did it take away from what I said?"

"No," I said. "I'm worried it hurt her feelings."

His mouth turned up on one side. "When Em approached me, she told me she wasn't looking for any feelings, anything serious. I never thought I would see you again, but for three years, I avoided committing to anyone. I knew I wouldn't be fully in it, not when I still wasn't over you. Trust me, she wasn't invested."

It was official. I didn't want any further details of what their time together entailed. My stomach wouldn't quite settle, knowing I'd have to be around Vance *and* the girl he was with so recently. It might take a while before I could stop comparing my looks to hers and wondering if he would feel like he made the wrong choice. But everybody had a past, just like Em told me. She had no reason to lie when she said that he looked at me with love, even back then. I clenched my fists, once each, urging myself to grab the doorknob.

The door swung open before I could convince my hands.

"Hey," Em said, looking straight at me with an open expression. "It's only weird if you make it weird."

With that, she grabbed my wrist and tugged me into the room. Vance followed and closed the door behind him.

I glanced at her bed, then at Em, then back at Vance.

Em didn't miss a thing. "Relax, we never went all the way," she said in that plain, dry way she had.

My eyes widened, and my cheeks flushed *again*. How was it possible that she said it never happened, but it was suddenly all I could think about?

Mink sat at the head of an unclaimed bed. Hudson sprawled along the bed with his head resting on Mink's lap, looking ready to fall asleep with heavy-lidded eyes as Mink slowly combed his fingers through Hudson's hair.

"Do we have to spend more time on the Vance and Tallie drama?" Julion asked, rolling his eyes. "It's been boring me for years already." He was sitting on the other empty bed, leaning against the wall and stretching his legs out.

Vance cleared his throat. "So, what's up?"

"Strategizing for tomorrow's test," Em replied, then turned her attention to me. "Any chance you'll give a semi-private lesson on how we work with fire?"

I chewed on my bottom lip, considering. "I don't know how closely they're watching me."

"You're being *watched*?" Hudson asked, sitting up, all signs of drowsiness gone from his features.

I nodded. "I'm probably not supposed to tell anyone that, either, but he never came out and forbade me from it."

"He? Who's watching you?" Hudson turned to Vance. "Did you know about this?"

Vance's jaw twitched, and it looked like he was grinding his teeth inside his closed mouth. He caught my look and softened slightly. "I knew the goons in suits had her in some tinted window car, and that something was wrong, but not what exactly."

"Director Hooper? Why the hell would he bother watching you?" Julion asked.

Em sat on the bed he had claimed and elbowed him. "Because Tallie not getting into the Oracus would make people doubt how accurate his Seers are." When she noticed my open-mouthed gape, she laughed. "What? I got curious about your past. It's a little juicier than the average contestant's."

"Okay," I said, surprised to be fine with her snooping through my life. "But I don't think I can talk about this with anyone, even if I'm not the one who let it slip. So can we not?"

"Why do you want to do what he says, anyway?" Em asked.

She must have missed that minute of my past.

"I think he's going to hurt my parents," I whispered through a full throat.

My mind replayed the prediction of that cold water; my parents discarded in its depths. What if the agents heard us talking right now? What if this conversation was the reason my parents might die? Before my breathing could run away with itself, I clung to my earlier conviction—the prediction was faulty. There was too much turmoil in me to focus, and I divined it wrong.

Still. I had to check.

I lunged for the door, opened it, and stepped into the empty hallway. No creepy agents or anyone else. A small wave of relief washed over me, but I couldn't get too relaxed. Direct eavesdropping was only *one* way they could keep tabs on my conversations.

Vance watched me curiously from the doorway until I stepped back inside Em's room.

"Can you do me a favor?" I asked her.

"What is it?"

I noticed she didn't agree without knowing the task, but I couldn't quite blame her for the hesitation.

"Can you look at my parents' past?" I asked. "Maybe yesterday, or this morning if you can? I want to see where they are, then I can warn them … Somehow." Another worry to add to the list—how to get a message out of the building while on lockdown.

"Yeah, I think I can do that," she said. "Do you have anything of theirs? It helps me focus if I've never met the person before. I mean, I saw them once or twice when reading your past, but the faces fade, you know?"

Nodding even though I didn't know, I walked to my box of belongings. I still hadn't made it to the bottom of the clothing. It was time to find out if my parents included anything personal or if they'd written me off. Their lone child, the failure.

"Let me check."

Reaching in, I grabbed a stack of folded clothes and set them aside on my bed, not caring when the pile toppled over. On the next reach, my hand hit the hard cover of a book. I pulled it out and my stomach sank. It was a first-year Foretold textbook—five hundred dry pages of rudimentary, beginning Seer knowledge. My parents must have thought I'd been denied entry to the Oracus because my skills weren't good enough. Never mind that I'd been the top student. Any failure was total failure.

"Sorry," I said to Em. It came out breathy and quiet. "I don't have anything."

With more force than was necessary, I threw the book onto the bed. It bounced, flipped, and landed wide open and face down. A white rectangle fluttered to the floor, freed from within the textbook's pages. I bent to pick it up, turned it over, then slid right to the floor when my brain processed what was in front of me.

It was a stained recipe card in familiar handwriting: *Stacey's Snickerdoodles*.

It unlocked a memory from before the Foretelling of my future. I was little, wearing a faded pink apron three sizes too big, with the words *pig out* embroidered on the front. My mom held me by the waist as I balanced on a kitchen stool to reach a bowl of dough held by my dad. Their faces came to mind, clearer than I could summon them before, and I became breathless, lost in the memory. They were *beaming* at me. Both of them had stared at me with wonder and pride, like I used to see Vance's parents shine toward their children every day. I suddenly remembered a hundred days like that before I was Foretold, with my dad teaching me his favorite parts of the culinary trade. We would use recipes from his sister, my Aunt Stacey. My mom loved watching, just spending that time together. Why hadn't I remembered them looking at me like that without it being attached to Elite status or my future as a Seer?

Maybe they could be happy with me, even if I wasn't Foretold.

If I quit the competition that minute and never stepped foot inside the Oracus, they might keep me in their lives and love me without condition when I found them. That wasn't an option, though, thanks to Director Hooper's warnings. Keeping them safe meant doing as I was told. The disappointment of that reality couldn't diminish the sensation of helium within my chest. I was light, buoyant, and soaring over the crushing expectations that had weighed me down for years. My parents might be proud of me for being me.

I hugged the paper to my chest and realized everyone in the room was silent and staring at me, aside from Mink. He had averted his eyes and was swatting at Hudson's chest, trying to draw his attention away from me.

I cleared my throat, got up from the floor, and handed the recipe to Em.

"It was my aunt's first, but my parents used it. Will it work?"

She looked it over and nodded. Closing her eyes while clutching the paper in one hand, she performed a series of breathing—a combination of short and long breaths with patterned pauses between. I felt like hyperventilating just witnessing it, but she eased into peacefulness before long. Every few seconds, a muscle twitch would cause her to jerk, but she was otherwise motionless. She woke from her trance and tried to hide the short, furtive glance she shot my way. But I noticed. She closed her eyes quickly, shook her head, and went through the breathing ritual again.

Vance made his way next to me and offered me his hand to hold. I ignored it, tucking myself close to his side instead. I peeked up to see wonder in his eyes and a smile that flashed across his face as he wrapped an arm around me. We waited together.

Em's second trance was shorter than the first. She shook her head and tried a third time. By then, I had trouble staying still. Even Julion looked twitchy. I didn't know if she always took that many attempts, or if there was a problem. I burrowed deeper into Vance's side, using his warmth to chase away the chill of my prediction about my parents.

Her eyes opened but she kept them glued to the floor. I'd never seen her look anything less than confident until that moment. My thumbnails snuck under the nails of my ring fingers, digging into the sensitive skin.

"I had to check a few times to be sure," she said.

Vance wrapped his other arm around my front, encircling me.

"I wanted to be absolutely sure," she added.

"Ugh, *tell* us already," Hudson demanded.

Em raised her eyes slowly until they met mine. "Tallie, they're already dead."

CHAPTER 25

I didn't cry.

I didn't move, aside from my mouth dropping open.

My internal organs kept moving on their own, I supposed, but I wasn't aware of anything. It was like my brain refused any input, just to avoid processing that one, impossible message.

They're already dead.

The only thing that jarred me out of stasis was Julion's voice, abrupt and unwelcome as always.

"How did they die?" he asked Em like it was any of his business.

She shook her head, shooting him a glare. Seemed like she agreed with me about it not being his business. Too bad his question was the same as mine.

"It's okay," I said. "I need to know."

"Are you sure?" Vance asked before Em had a chance to reply.

I nodded my head, knowing he'd feel it since I was still pressing myself into him.

"A couple of agents went to your house after the Oracus ceremony." Em's dry tone fit the situation perfectly.

If it had dripped with sympathy, I would've broken down before I could hear the whole story.

She carried on in her factual, detached report, "They had your parents pack a box for you, then tried to get them to leave the house. Your mom refused. Said she didn't trust what was happening and demanded to see you."

Em stopped talking to look at me closely.

I waved her on, my throat too full to speak.

"They grabbed your mom. She fought back and one of them pinned her to the ground. Handcuffed her. Your dad pulled a gun on him. The other man came from behind and got it away from him. He shot both of your parents. It happened so fast. The men carried them out of the house, and that's all I saw."

It was enough. I peeled away from Vance's side. "Excuse me," I said, my voice so calm it was eerie, even to myself. I walked to the door and stepped out into the hallway.

Vance came out right after me. "What are you going to do?" he asked quietly, like the walls weren't thin and no one in Em's room could hear.

I started walking down the hallway, picking up my pace with every step. "I'm going to kill Hooper's goons. I don't care which ones shot my parents; they're all going down."

Vance ran to get ahead, then turned to face me, walking backward and slowing my pace.

"How?" he asked.

I paused in my determined stride.

"They deserve it, don't get me wrong," he said, "but do you know how to kill a trained agent of the directorate?"

I shook my head, confused by the sudden urge to turn my rage against Vance. I pushed past him and continued stalking down the hallway.

"Tallie, you're going to get *yourself* killed. We just found each other again. *Please*." His voice broke. "I'll help you; I'll help you with anything but stop and think this through."

I stopped and turned.

He stood where I had left him behind, both of his hands fisted in his hair, his eyes were wide and wild with something bigger than fear.

I walked back the way I came, advancing on him slowly. "I don't want to think. Thinking is the worst thing I could do right now. If I stop to think, I have to come to terms with what Em's vision showed. It would make me accept a reality that I. Just. Can't." I reached Vance and tilted my chin up to stare into his eyes. "So why would you ask me to stop and think?"

"Because I love you," he whispered.

The tears I had been holding back flooded my eyes and spilled over. A torrent of pain poured out of me, almost knocking me to the floor. Vance caught me and hefted me up in his arms until I was tucked against his chest, where I muffled my cries. He carried me to his room, somehow opening the door without letting go of me, and he didn't put me down when we got inside. He walked to his bed and sat down, still with me cradled in his arms.

We stayed like that until my tears had run out and I was no longer gasping out soundless sobs. He laid down on his side, so my back rested on the bed, where I remained tucked to his chest. His lips found my forehead where he brushed kiss after gentle, slow kiss until he stopped moving his lips away and rested his face on top of my head.

I sniffed in, trying heroically and ineffectually to rein in my running nose. Vance leaned back from me, gripped his shirt behind his back, and pulled it over his head in one smooth movement. It was hard to blame him, with how wet I'd made it.

Vance handed me his shirt. "Blow your nose on this."

I stared at him to check his conviction about the idea. The blues of his eyes were guileless. Only caring shone through. I dabbed around my eyes first, blew my nose, then leaned over to drop the soiled shirt to the floor.

The door creaked open.

"Uh, is this really the appropriate time to be getting naked, man?"

Julion. Of course, it was Julion interrupting my grief.

"I just came in to say you should've let her go after the assholes," he explained after, I assumed, Vance made some sort of face at him.

It should have been impossible, but I laughed. The sound cut off sharply as I worried it was a betrayal to my parents and wondered how the sound came from me at all in the wake of devastation.

Seemingly encouraged, Julion walked further into the room and sat on his bed. "Seriously, who wouldn't want to see the world's biggest apologizer lose it on some dudes twice her size?" he asked. "What she lacks in training, I bet she makes up for with repressed rage."

That did it. The laughter came again, not caring that it was wholly inappropriate for the moment. When it died away, a long time later, I realized it had taken with it part of the weight that my tears had failed to relieve.

Vance was right there next to me through all of it. I knew he wouldn't judge me for laughing like I was insane right after bawling all over him. Julion's opinion of me didn't matter, though his smirk was tinged with approval.

"What are we going to do?" Vance asked.

"We as in …" Since we weren't alone, I wasn't sure who he wanted included in my planning.

"All of us," Vance said.

I looked to Julion who nodded, sans a rude comment. Huh. Maybe being *with* Vance earned me a pass. Something about that stung.

"I don't really have a plan for 'we,'" I said. "For me, I'm leaving the competition. I started it to make my parents proud of me again. I stayed in because Director Hooper threatened them if I didn't. Now, I have no reason to do anything he asks."

"So that's what that day was about. When they took you away in their car. You were getting threatened?" Vance asked. He sat up, careful not to jostle me off the bed in doing so. "I don't have a reason to stay, either. I only did it to get my mom treatment."

My heart ached at the reminder of Gina's fate. I sat up, too. "What do you think they'll do if people start dropping out? Half the reason Hooper ordered me to win was so the validity of his Seers wouldn't be questioned after the Oracus gates didn't let me in."

"*That's* what happened?" Julion broke in. "Rumor went around that you changed your mind about being a Seer and refused to go in."

I shook my head. "That's Hooper's spin. Becoming a Seer was all I was ever supposed to do. Trying to walk into the Oracus and literally bouncing off a gate ward was, I thought, the worst thing that ever happened to me. Now I know how naïve that was."

"Wow," Julion said. "We thought you ditched us for something you ended up not even caring about."

"She didn't have the choice to keep hanging out with us," Vance said. "Her parents found out and put her on lockdown."

"Huh." Julion rubbed his jaw lightly, staring at a blank spot on the wall. "Assumptions, assholes, and all that."

"It might be too dangerous for you to leave the competition," Vance said.

"The other reason Hooper wants me to win is because he thinks I respond well to threats. Apparently, that's a quality he looks for in a Seer." I blushed and looked away, not wanting to witness their realization of my weakness. "He's been having us predict the outcome of the nations that are outlawing Seers so I would think I had it good here. He kind of insinuated that if I wasn't cooperative, he'd ship me off to one of those nations."

The bed started to shake. I looked over and saw Vance's leg bouncing up and down quickly.

"I mean, it's up to you," he said, "but you can't risk that, right? You should stay in the competition."

"Unless we escape," Julion said. His head whipped to the door when the knob turned.

At the same time, Vance sprang from the bed, stepping in front of me.

Em, Hudson, and Mink came in and quickly shut the door behind them.

"We're escaping?" Mink asked, his eyebrows raised. "Can we do that with Vance's parents and sister here?"

"No, we're not escaping," Vance said, sitting down beside me again.

"Not yet," I amended.

Five heads swiveled to stare at me. The flutter of possibility took up the dark, empty space where the hope for my parents' lives used to reside.

"They're expecting us for the test in the morning," I said, then glanced to the window. "It's evening already; we can't exactly plan a way to sneak everyone past the agents before then. So, we do the test in the morning. Before that, though, we plan. And then we get out of here, away from where Hooper can threaten or," I swallowed hard, "kill us if we don't do what he wants."

"Hell yeah," Julion said calmly, relaxing back against his headboard.

Hudson and Em nodded along, but Mink and Vance both wore worried expressions.

I turned to Vance and splayed my palm over his thigh, hoping to reassure him. "We won't do anything that will put your parents or Liann in danger," I said, firmly committed to that promise. "But I won't work for Hooper as a Seer, predicting what he wants or risk dying. I'm sorry, but we have to go."

"I know," Vance said in a thick whisper. "But I'm scared."

That had my eyes widening. Vance was up for literally anything anyone suggested when we were younger, always ready for adventure and having fun by taking stupid risks. Not once had he ever admitted fear.

"I'm scared, too," I told him truthfully.

Vance shook his head. "I'm scared for *you*. You're on the Director's radar, and he isn't going to let you go easily."

CHAPTER 26

Vance didn't want to let me go, either, but I managed to convince him that an escape attempt made on a full night of sleep was a successful escape attempt. I spent the night listening to Em's light snoring until drifting into a broken, uneasy sleep.

He, Em, and I convened with Maddoc and Kinsley—the other two remaining contestants—in the living room just before nine o'clock. Granger was already there, stoking the fire that burned my divining sticks in the fireplace. The camerawoman stared into a screen at the back of her device, pressing buttons with an impassive expression.

"Can't we watch?" Mink's voice filtered in from the hallway. "We won't make a sound."

"Yeah, you guys are trapping us here," Hudson agreed. "The least you can do is entertain us."

The agent they appealed to finally said, "I suggest you abandon the idea of entertainment. Now disappear."

I rose from the couch, ready to intervene on behalf of my friends. How, I wasn't sure, but the growly threat in the agent's words dropped a heavy lump in my stomach.

"Disappear in *this* kind of weather?" Hudson asked, but from the apathetic faintness, his heart wasn't in the attempt. Footsteps headed away from the living room, and I sat down again, letting the unease in my stomach slowly settle.

Granger straightened from stooping over the fireplace and leaned the poker against the brick mantle. He clasped his hands in front of his waist and narrowed his eyes at each of us in turn. He'd blossomed from the nervous wreck we had first met. It was too bad.

"Today," he said, "you will be tested on the future you divine from reading these flames. In the same vein as your previous test, I ask you to predict the announcement of how many Seers died after the nation of Arizona rendered them illegal. The announcement is scheduled to be made this evening, so we must have all predictions completed beforehand, while the answer still lies in the future."

I blew out a long breath, trying to keep it quiet to avoid attention. I didn't want to predict the report of this devastation that had likely already occurred. I was unable to stop any of it. Seerdom was all I aspired to for so long, but the recent past had shown me how utterly useless it was. I didn't care if I ever predicted anything for the rest of my life.

Vance was called to go first. At least I wouldn't have to intervene to keep Em in the running this time, assuming she still wanted to win. Maybe there'd be a chance someday to ask her why.

Vance approached the fireplace, stared at the flames for approximately three seconds, then turned his back. He wrote his answer, handed it to Granger, then returned to my side.

I knew he had written a random number. He'd told me this morning that it was safe for him to lose the competition, so he'd throw it.

Kinsley was called. I hadn't seen her since she accused me of having Ethyl's blood on my hands, and I didn't hold it against her. She approached the fireplace without making eye contact with anyone and settled on the floor in front of it, cross-legged. Maybe she wanted to make up for Vance's flippant turn, because she stayed put for at least fifteen minutes, staring at the flames, trying to divine their message. Or maybe she was lost in memories of her friend and not actually seeing the dancing flames in front of her.

I spent that time staring at the agent in the room with us, wondering if he had been the one to pull the trigger, to end my parents' lives.

Maddoc was more reasonable with the length of his reading, capping it at a couple minutes. I wondered if he truly had Seer talent, or if another unknown ability had gotten him this far in the contest. Then it was Em's turn.

She stood in front of the fireplace, going through her breathing pattern. After only a moment, she turned and shot a quizzical look at

Vance with her eyebrows scrunched up and that one fine wrinkle appearing on her nose. I wondered what absurdly wrong number he had written down that made her react that way. Em returned her focus to the fireplace, did her breathing again, then left to write down her answer.

It was my turn. I needed to make an accurate prediction, to keep myself safe until we were able to escape. But the thought of seeking out the details of more death sent a wave of shivers through me. There was no hiding them. Everyone surely saw me trembling.

I approached the fireplace, considering my options, though I knew I had only one. Which meant I had no options at all. Standing in the warmth of the hearth, I saw the sticks were nearly all blackened. Some of the ends had already crumbled to ash. The flames danced over them, swaying and sparking. Taunting. I formed the question in my mind. How many Seer deaths in Arizona will be announced today?

My brain began to interpret the movement of the flames, and I squeezed my eyes shut, cutting off the message. No. I wouldn't read it. The consequences didn't matter; those were *my* sticks. I almost fell out of a tree to get them, trimmed them, touched them all over, and became familiarized with their essence. Though it would do nothing to change anyone's circumstances, I couldn't let my materials deliver a message of death.

I opened my eyes and reached for the long poker. I shoved it into the firepit, shifting the remains of my sticks and altering the movement and position of the flames. Something itched in one side of my mind as I monitored the fiery changes.

A hand wrenched the poker from my grasp, and I stumbled back a step. Granger held the poker behind his back, his brow furrowed, and his chin tucked in, like I had personally affronted him.

"You may not use any additional materials in this test. This is your only warning before disqualifi—" he broke off, distracted by one of the agents. He cleared his throat, licked his lips, and, more quietly, amended his statement, "This is a warning."

I fumed in silence. Like this man knew anything about divination. Like he knew anything about the people who would suffer, whose fates we were exploiting to provide Director Hooper with more faithful servants. I turned my back on Granger to stare at the flames.

The message was coming in differently than before, but it was still not what I wanted.

I walked forward in a daze until my toes crossed the edge of the hearth, inches from the burning sticks. No additional materials, he said. Well, my body wasn't a material. I crouched low, ignoring the stray sparks that singed my knees.

I reached into the flames and moved a blackened, crumbling stick with my bare hand, barely cringing at the searing heat, not when the itch was back in the right side of my brain, growing in intensity. Frowning, I considered the result. Not right, not yet. I reached in further, pushing and pulling at the sticks' positions, still so familiar to me in their natural essence, even when they were halfway to being embers.

A vague receptor inside me took note of the exclamations and protests ringing through the room. The itching in my mind grew to a burning, more noticeable than the physical flames before me. A hand grabbed my arm, and I shook it off. Just one more move, and—there.

I scooted back, holding my bright red hand away from the fire, keeping it farther from any additional heat, but I stared into the flames and nodded as the itch in my mind receded. The message read what it should have all along if I were allowed to plan the future. I rose to standing and walked stiffly to where the paper and pencil waited. With my unburned hand, I wrote a large zero on the paper, then handed it to the officiant.

As soon as my answer was provided, Vance swooped in behind me and pushed me toward the hallway. Still partially dazed, I allowed him to steer me down the hall, through the foyer, and into the kitchen.

He ran ahead and turned on the faucet, letting the cold water run at full blast. I followed him and stuck my hand in the stream, wincing at the jarring contact.

"What happened?" Julion asked.

I hadn't noticed he was in the kitchen already, closing the refrigerator door.

"She stuck her hand in the fire," Vance said, a little too loudly for the size of the room.

"Let me see," Julion said. He squeezed between Vance and the counter to stand next to me.

I tried to ignore the cringe on his face as he assessed the damage to my hand. My head was somewhere in a partial daydream of a different future—one in which Seers were not being eradicated—and the image kept me separated from the pain.

Julion turned away almost immediately and returned to the refrigerator. So much for thinking we might be friends again, now that Vance and I were together. The freezer door opened and shut in a matter of seconds. Vance let Julion reclaim the spot by my side. He reached out his hand for mine.

I looked at Vance, like he could help me understand Julion's intentions. All he did was nod and smile tightly. With a sigh, I pulled my hand from the cold water and held it in front of Julion.

He grasped my wrist, at the point where the burn marks stopped. In his other hand, he held an ice cube with his finger and thumb. Staring intently at my hand, he pressed the ice to it, while simultaneously massaging the fingers of his other hand into my wrist. The daydream, that aching impossibility of no more death, burst and I returned fully to the present.

The ice melted faster than it had any right to. It dripped off the sides of my hand and puddled on the floor in the span of a few seconds. Julion held on, still pressing his fingers into my wrist. My hand paled from the angry red color to a less concerning pink. Julion released me and stepped back, breathing heavily.

I looked from him to Vance, then back again. It shouldn't have been possible, but he healed me. Not completely—there was still discomfort in my hand, and the color wasn't quite right—but it was a far cry from what it had looked like when Vance first brought me into the kitchen. He somehow took a blistering, ruinous injury, and turned it into a minor ache.

"How long have you known you could do that?" Vance asked.

Julion shrugged. "Kind of forever. My parents scared me into keeping it a secret. Something about an old friend of theirs disappearing after going public with a talent like that." He turned to me. "It shouldn't blister. Sorry I couldn't get it any better."

I gaped, mouth all the way open. "Are you kidding? *Thank* you. I didn't even think about hurting my hand, it just—it just kind of happened."

Vance eyed my hand but refrained from touching it. "Do you know *why* you did that?"

"I wanted a different answer," I said quietly, then changed the subject before slipping back into my daydream. "What number did you write down? Em gave you the weirdest look."

Vance chuckled. "Zero," he said. "It was the only acceptable answer."

Keeping my pink hand out to the side to avoid bumping it, I reached my good hand up around his neck, stood on my toes, and pulled him down for a kiss. I meant for it to be short, but Vance's mouth followed mine when I started to pull back, so I gave in and lingered in the joy and the disbelief and the heat that consumed me whenever we kissed.

When we broke apart, Julion had left the kitchen. I cringed a little.

Vance laughed it off. "He's fine. Just being unusually polite."

"You didn't know he could heal people?" I asked.

Vance shook his head. "It explains why he was so broken up about Ethyl's death, though."

I wrinkled my nose at him. "How could you tell? Em slapped him for *joking* about it."

"That's just how he comes off on the surface," Vance said. "He was mad. Like seething, deep anger. I'd have to ask to be sure, but now I think he was pissed that he didn't save her life."

"Electrocution is a little different from burnt skin," I said, considering the aftermath of Ethyl's death from a new angle.

Vance nodded his agreement and pulled me close to his chest. I sank against his solid frame, reliving the moment he had carried Ethyl into the dormitory and when I realized she was dead. I didn't stay in his comforting hold for long. We would have a lifetime, hopefully a long one, to mourn the dead. But there was someone still alive who could use our time first.

"Can we go see your parents?" I asked.

Vance nodded, and we walked together to their first-floor wing, the ghosts of my mom and dad following—two deaths I couldn't push aside, no matter the urgency of the present.

CHAPTER 27

"Tallie!" Gina exclaimed before she acknowledged her own son. She rocked back and forth two times before pushing herself up from the couch to hug me. Maybe it was my imagination, but she breathed more heavily than normal with each step she took.

I caught Peter's eye over her shoulder, and he pressed his lips together tightly, shaking his head.

"How did we get so lucky to see *both* of you at the *same time*?" she asked, wiggling her eyebrows to excess.

Vance smiled and grabbed her in a hug. "Because we talked like regular people and realized we didn't have to be apart for the past three years." His tone was light, infused with a laugh. "I'm planning on being around her as much as she'll let me."

My heart skipped at least two beats and I silently admonished it, not sure if it was appropriate to be so happy about something with grief all around.

Gina swatted her hand at me, not making contact. "Don't you dare hold back that smile, you sweet girl. If everyone cries around me all the time, I won't just be sick, I'll be miserable."

"It's true," Peter said. "The best thing you can do is surround her with things that have nothing to do with cancer."

"He's finally catching on," Gina teased. "I only had to tell him five hundred and three times. Lucky for you, Tallie, Vance usually takes after me when it comes to catching on to hints."

"He missed all of mine three years ago," I said, then clapped a hand over my mouth, not quite believing that I said that in front of his parents. "Sorry," I squeaked.

Vance leaned down to whisper in my ear. "You've always been an exception to every rule." His lips skipped from my ear to press against my cheek that was surely flaming red.

Gina and Peter shared teary-eyed smiles, then ushered us all the way into the living room to sit and visit.

Liann's bedroom door flew open, and she rolled out in a wheelchair.

"Are you *kidding* me?" she screeched. "All that angst and drama and now you look like you've been together forever." She smiled but pointed a stern finger our way. "No fair being cute when I can't see my husband for who knows how long."

"Sorry," I said, putting my hands in the air.

Vance tucked an arm around my back. "I promise nothing," he said, then released me and crossed the room to hug his sister.

She accepted the hug, then smacked him lightly on the arm. He pretended it hurt; in their show I'd seen so many times before. He backed away slowly, really playing it up, and returned to the couch. Liann pushed against the large wheels on her chair but didn't move. She tried again, straining against the stationary wheelchair. The couch cushion vibrated with Vance's concealed laugh.

"Ugh, Vance," she complained, then freed the brakes he had surreptitiously locked while he hugged her.

After everyone was settled, Vance stopped joking and looked at his parents with grim-set eyes. "Are they mistreating you?"

Peter shook his head. "We barely see the agents. It's almost like being at home. Except, well, not at all."

Gina leaned over the arm of her chair to pat his leg.

I caught Vance's eye, wondering if we should warn them of what the director's agents were capable of. Vance shook his head minutely. I'd have to ask him later why he didn't want them to know about my parents yet.

The next two hours were spent in a state of suspended reality. It burst with the feelings of comfort their home gave me when I was younger. I had always wished for a family like theirs but stopped short of envy. It was how things were, and even then, I realized circumstances would never change for me. I had hoped they'd never change for the Oleskis. That was one daydream that came true, aside from Gina's cancer.

Was there any happiness allowed to pass through life unscathed and unpunished for its purity?

Vance and I grabbed something to eat from the dormitory kitchen afterward for an early lunch. I didn't know how fresh food kept appearing every day. It was hard to imagine any of the agents on a mundane errand like grocery shopping. The more I watched them, the more obvious it was that they were trained and geared for intimidation, brute force, and government-sanctioned murders.

But they were still human. They had to use the bathroom, eat, drink, sleep. Was there always someone covering for them for the smallest of breaks? Or were there times in the day or night when the exit wasn't being guarded?

Loud, repeated banging came from the direction of the foyer. Though muffled through the walls, multiple people were yelling. Vance and I shared a wide-eyed look, then almost as one, ran to the foyer. I skidded to a stop in disbelief.

Vance continued running straight to the window, where his older siblings were visible on the other side. Two of his sisters had their hands cupped to the glass, peering through. Nearby, three of his brothers and another sister banged their fists against the glass, yelling demands for entrance into the building.

Two agents stood in front of the door; their arms crossed. It didn't matter how much commotion Vance's family caused, there was no way any of them could unlock or break down the door and then make it past the suited goons. My breath hitched in my throat as I stared at the agents and tried not to imagine them restraining and shooting my parents. They couldn't do that to anyone in Vance's family. Where was the line his siblings would have to cross to be shot? What would change them from mere nuisances to being perceived threats to Director Hooper's power?

I marched to the nearest agent and cleared my throat, announcing my presence. He didn't budge. Not even the twitch of an eye to check me in his periphery.

"Excuse me," I said, mustering some force behind my voice, to be heard over the Oleski disturbance. "I need to talk to Director Hooper."

I stuffed down the urge to apologize for being demanding. These men didn't deserve my habitual word, but I still averted my eyes.

Vance turned his head from the window, where he'd been mouthing some sort of silent message to his sisters. He narrowed his eyes at the agent who was busy ignoring me.

"Hey," he called, his deeper voice taking up more of the space in the room than mine could. "The lady is talking to you."

The agent finally turned to face me.

"I need to talk to Director Hooper," I repeated with less conviction. Being ignored until a male advocated for me was a free-flowing drain on confidence, no matter who he was.

The agent lifted one eyebrow, but otherwise didn't react.

"There's something he needs to know," I said, gaining volume, "and if he finds out one of you kept his new soon-to-be-Seer from informing him, he's not going to be thrilled."

The agent sighed, waited a moment, then responded, "He'll be here soon."

Within the next two minutes, the silver car pulled up to the curb in front of the building. The agent who had spoken to me opened the door and shoved me outside. I stumbled forward a few steps before regaining my balance. The door shut firmly behind me before Vance's family could squeeze their way in.

"Tallie?" one of Vance's sisters asked incredulously. "What the hell is going on?"

"Sorry," I said, over and over, as I ignored their questions and rushed to the car. The door opened from the inside. I ducked in, pulling the door shut behind me. The car screeched away from the curb before I had a chance to click my buckle in place.

Director Hooper glowered at me from his side of the back seat. "I don't particularly enjoy being summoned," he said. "What's the information you have?"

He knew what I'd said to the agent, but the man hadn't radioed for the director at all. How had he passed along the information? There had to be recording devices in the building, monitored by more of Hooper's men. A chill ran from my right shoulder to my left. If they were present in the bedrooms, the agents knew we were planning an escape.

I swallowed the nervous lump in my throat. If there was ever a time to mimic Em's confidence, it was now.

"The family that you're keeping in the dormitory with us, the Oleskis, how much do you know about them?"

Hooper inclined his head toward me with a withering stare. "More than I would care to know. Mainly that they are in possession of knowledge that can't be made public, or it might interfere with the selection of new Seers."

"The people making a scene back there are their children and not even all of them," I said, fighting to control the shaking in my limbs. "They keep close tabs on each other. If you didn't let Peter and Gina give their kids a cover story before taking them, they know something is up."

"Are you suggesting I collect the entire family? It can be arranged."

"No!" I cleared my throat and took a steadying breath. "The other thing you may not know, is that they are the best people."

"They're Pedestrians," he said, like that was a complete refutation.

I ignored him. "Everyone thinks they're the best. They know their entire neighborhood, and all of their children are just as well liked. These are people who can't disappear. *Everyone* who's even remotely in their lives will notice. And if their kids don't leave with their parents and sister today, they'll get reinforcements and come back tomorrow. Then anyone who passes by will see a mob and get curious. And you're going to have to figure out how to publicly justify kidnapping a cancer-stricken woman and her pregnant daughter who's supposed to be on bed rest." I was breathing heavily, recovering from the rush of the words that had poured out of me with desperate frustration.

Hooper pinned his gaze straight ahead, eyes tensely narrowed. There was one final suggestion he needed to hear, but I worried I'd already pushed too hard.

"For the Oleskis," I said, "just having their son in this competition and under the watch of your agents would be enough for them to keep any secret you want them to. They'd never put one of their children in danger, no matter what."

Pretending to be confident and asserting myself for that long took its toll. I sank back against the door, my usual pose in the director's car. Ugh. I had a "usual" when it came to the director. There was a day, not long ago, when I would have marveled over that circumstance. The age of marveling was over. It was time for anger and action.

The ride was silent, bristling, until we pulled up to the dormitory. As I suspected, Vance's siblings were still hard at work, disrupting the exterior.

An agent opened my door and beckoned me out. I'd take that over being yanked around, but if they thought they would receive a thank you card, they'd be waiting a very long time. I stepped toward the building, but the agent held out his arm in front of me.

Vance's brother noticed us and approached swiftly. "What's going on in there? What are they doing with Mom and Dad and Liann?"

I peeked at the agent from the corner of my eye. He didn't shoot any looks of warning my way. "They're okay so far," I said, knowing I shouldn't push it, not if I wanted the entire Oleski family to go free.

Vance's sisters and another brother joined us. All but one of his sisters stared at me with their mouths pinched shut. The other sister stepped forward.

"What are you doing all cozy with the guys who *kidnapped* our family?" she asked, looking me up and down.

"I'm sorry," I said, knowing it looked bad, and also knowing I couldn't get specific enough to sate their suspicions. "I'm not cozy at all."

She snorted and turned her back on me, returning to pound on the building's doors and windows as the director's car pulled away. I got treated to a whole range of emotions from the remaining Oleski siblings. One by one, they shot me either withering glares, mournful looks of regret, disappointed shakes of the head, or pure confusion.

Someday, with luck, Gina and Peter, Liann, or even Vance could set them straight about my involvement with Hooper. For now, I had to endure their assumptions.

The door swung open, and Vance's sister had to jump back to avoid getting hit. A bristling agent stormed outside with more emotion than I'd ever witnessed from one of them. Following behind were Gina, Peter, and an agent pushing Liann's wheelchair. Liann was in an almost perpetual loop of rolling her eyes at her siblings. Gina had a glazed look in her eyes like she was in some kind of shock from her turn of circumstance. Peter kept his eyes on his two most vulnerable girls, making sure to stay within arms' reach of them both.

For my part, I gaped at the scene. That happened so fast. Maybe it was Director Hooper's plan all along, and it was coincidence that I had advised him to free the Oleski family ten minutes before their release.

Vance's family lost themselves in simultaneous conversations and exclamations. This was how I remembered them; busy, chaotic, loving. Perfect. I couldn't spy on their reunion for long because another agent took me by the elbow to steer me through the door and into the foyer. Vance waited there, watching his family through the window. He turned to me with misty eyes.

"Did you make this happen?" he asked, breathless, eyes wide.

I shrugged. "I suggested it, but he was probably already planning to let them leave because it happened so fast—"

I never finished brushing off the credit, because Vance wrapped his arms around my waist and lifted me off the floor. He spun us once, then pressed a kiss to my lips that seared, then lingered. My head swam in clouds, but not from the spinning. I laid my palms against his cheeks and accepted the physical gratitude better than I ever could if it was spoken out loud. After too short of a time, he eased me down until my feet touched the floor. I stepped away and wavered in my balance for a moment. When I regained my sense of place, I noticed two agents in the foyer pointedly staring away from us.

"I should probably confess something before you kiss me like that again," I said.

Vance waited patiently but looked like he might interrupt and kiss me anyway.

"When I asked Hooper to let your parents and Liann go, I pointed out that he'd still have you for collateral. I told him your family would keep anything quiet if it would keep you safe. I might have put your life in danger, and I'm sorry, but I had to get your family out of here."

Vance started shaking his head halfway through my speech. "Hey, no, don't feel like that's a confession." He ran his hands from my shoulders to my wrists, then back up again. "What you did was perfect. Getting them away from," he gestured at the agents with a thumb, "was the most important thing."

"I kind of put the fear of the Oleski neighborhood watch into him," I said with a sly smile.

Vance laughed out loud. "Anyone with a trace of brain matter would be afraid to cross them. So, what do you want to do to kill time before the broadcast?"

My answer should have been related to planning our escape, mourning my parents, *something* deeper than what I actually said.

"Want to see if anyone's in your room?"

Vance's eyebrows twitched slightly as he caught my meaning. "I want to see if anyone's *not* in my room."

Laughing, we raced up the stairs, down the hallway, and barreled into his room. Not only was Julion there, but so were Em, Hudson, and Mink. Everyone's heads jerked up when we burst through the door.

"Vance's family got to go home," I said in a rush, face burning. Maybe they'd believe that news was the reason we'd rushed in. Not that I wanted to kiss Vance for an extended, uninterrupted period of forgetting everything that was wrong.

Em snorted a laugh, earning her a playful shove from Mink.

"That's great," he said, full of warmth.

Hudson leaned forward, grinning. "I think it's great how obviously we're interrupting Vallie time and Tallie's going to fall all over herself pretending otherwise. In three … two …"

"We really wanted to tell you the news," I tried, the attempt sounding lame even to my ears. "Never mind. What's Vallie?"

"Vance and Tallie," Em explained. "These two," she waved a hand at Hudson and Mink, "wanted first dibs on your couple name."

My eyes widened in alarm. I looked at Vance.

"Did you …" There was no tactful way to ask if he and Em had a couple name.

Em stood from her seat, marched up to me, and placed her hands firmly on my shoulders. She bent slightly to match my height and stared into my eyes until I was squirming to break gazes.

"There was never really a Vance and me," she said slowly. "It was nothing. You guys are chronic. Terminal, even."

"I *hope* not," Hudson said.

"Shut up," Em said, barely sparing him a sideways glance. She focused on me. "I mean, you're it until the end, and I'm here for it." She released her grip and gave each of my shoulders a single, light pat. "Man, have fun with that level of insecurity," she stage-whispered to Vance before giving me a not-unkind smile.

I couldn't help the laughter that overwhelmed me. The embarrassment, then the elation of hearing someone think Vance and I were the real thing, the looming grief over my parents, Gina's diagnosis … Through it all, I still found time to worry over Vance's past relationships. Sure, I was eighteen, but this life was a *lot* and I suddenly, desperately wanted to still feel like a kid. I laughed harder when I noticed everyone staring at me, then harder still—holding my stomach, doubling over, losing my breath. Streaming tears, even.

"Ooh, is this crazy Tallie?" Hudson laughed in solidarity. "I can hang with this."

A firm, warm hand rubbed slow circles on my back. Vance had to wonder if I was going to devolve from laughter into devastation or panic, and I had the same concern. But searching within, nothing bubbled up but more hysterical laughter. At some point, my brain had decided to take a holiday, and I wouldn't deny it the pleasure. I hadn't taken one single break from focus and responsibility in three years. Enough was enough.

"Tallie," Vance said, and the extra weight of my name on his tongue danced up my spine in a chill that curbed my laughter. "You good?"

I straightened, wiping my eyes and catching a small portion of my breath. Em's mouth was stretched into an amused smile. Hudson kept chuckling, and Mink was doing his best to cover his boyfriend's mouth. Julion had one eyebrow cocked as he eyed the door. Vance's eyes danced with light, and I wanted to keep it there.

"Are you guys up for some fun?" I asked.

CHAPTER 28

That afternoon tested my theory that as long as we were contained indoors and not revealing any of Hooper's secrets, the rules were fairly lax. Our group crowded the foyer, took up positions around the room, and posed exactly like the agent in place. The winner was the last one standing without moving or making a sound. Em and Julion stuck as the final two until Hudson complained about being bored and wanting to move onto the next challenge. We played Try Not To Laugh, The Agent Edition. Working in pairs, we mimed comedy sketches inches from where the agent stood. He never strayed from his veneer of bored professionalism.

It was pointless, childish, and a waste of time. It was also nostalgic and wholly necessary, applying a few fresh patches to the cracks in my soul.

The effects fizzled that evening in the living room. The fireplace sat dim, only containing the ashen remains of my divination sticks. I sat on a couch next to Vance. Mink sat on my other side, with Hudson squeezed in at the end. Julion opted for a chair, as did Em, and Kinsley and Maddoc shared a couch, though they left an empty cushion between them.

Granger flipped on the radio, then stood by with two agents—different from the one we'd messed with earlier—as the static played. The first blurb of news had nothing to do with a nation banning its Seers.

"Director Hooper is hailed as an unsung hero, as his efforts to house an ailing family and provide them with Elite-level medical care were denied. In his trademark respectful manner, he has chosen to honor their refusal and provide transportation back to their chosen residence."

A tickle of breath preceded Vance's whisper in my ear. "Doesn't sucking up on the news make him a *sung* hero?"

If I was willing to risk the attention of the agents, I would have replied with a joke about the director's "trademark respectful manner." As it was, I was too tense about the coming announcement to feel much like joking. I hadn't allowed the flames to deliver their message to me about this future before I rearranged the sticks, but the essence of it had started to form. I suspected the number would be higher, much higher, than any we had heard before.

The broadcast continued:

"The nation of Arizona enacted a new law today, declaring all divination activities illegal." There was a long pause before the announcer resumed speaking, this time in a dazed, hesitant voice. "This resulted in zero deaths."

Someone in the room let loose with a high-pitched, unhinged laugh. Me. Omen's asshole, it was me. I clamped a still-pink hand over my mouth and tried to ignore the looks everyone gave me.

How could it be zero? The flames would have shown a large number of deaths, had I read them fully. Was that accurate, or had my fears clouded the unformed prediction? No—when I manipulated the sticks, the answer had changed. It wasn't going to be zero before that. Either my initial divination path was mistaken, or the future had changed.

An ache built deep in my brain. This was too much to decode. I dropped my hand and looked around for other reactions. The agents appeared slightly more tense than usual, but it was hard to tell. Granger spent a long minute clearing his throat and adjusting his collar.

"With this revelation of a broadcast," he said, staring at the form where he recorded our answers, "we have two contestants remaining in the competition. Which means, we have our winners."

My stomach staged an untimely upheaval, and I struggled to keep its contents where they belonged. Beside me, Vance went completely rigid.

"Vance Oleski and Natalie Kowalczyk, you will be admitted to the Oracus to complete your training as Seers."

No.

No, that couldn't be possible. I created my own answer, the wrong answer, on purpose. Vance hadn't even bothered to read the flames before giving his nonsense answer to the test. We were going to *escape*. His family had left the dormitory, so we were free to run without putting them in danger. Director Hooper had my parents *killed*. There wasn't a chance I could work for him, enduring more of his threats so I would comply with his whims, all the while knowing what he had done to my family.

An agent stepped forward to whisper in Granger's ear.

The officiant nodded, then relayed the message to the rest of us:

"Vance and Natalie, you will be escorted to the Oracus today. The rest of you are excused back to your homes or dormitories."

"It's not fair!" Em wailed, taking everyone by surprise.

She stood from the couch and bolted out of the room, shoulders heaving with loud sobs. Vance stared at the doorway she exited through, wide-eyed and incredulous. He looked back at me, but I shook my head, just as clueless as he was. Em had never shown that level of emotion in front of me before. I wouldn't be surprised if she'd never done that in her life. My stomach burned with guilt. There must have been a deeper reason for her to seek out Seerdom, and Vance and I were taking positions she wanted more desperately than I had realized. Silence stretched through the room in her wake as Kinsley and Maddoc left slowly and sedately.

They both had their reasons for seeking Seerdom. I'd never know the specifics, but the possibilities would haunt me. I could only hope they weren't depending on Elite status for something urgent or life-saving. It was too late for Gina, and too late for my parents. Would someone in their lives, or in Em's, suffer because I won the competition?

"Are we leaving immediately?" I asked, pressing my hands, one pink and one pale, over my queasy stomach.

"There is time to pack your belongings," Granger replied. "In one hour, a car will be out front to collect you."

I didn't need any further permission. I stood, tugging Vance's hand with barely restrained urgency, and we hastened out of the living room. My stomach coiled in on itself more with each step toward Em's room, uncertain how I would console her, afraid of the state I'd find her in. Vance had rejected her because of me. The Oracus had rejected her in favor of me. If she hated me, I'd have to agree with her.

It took three deep breaths before I could turn the doorknob and walk into her room.

"Took you long enough," Em said, lounging on her bed. "We've already started planning."

Her eyes were dry, not a hint of redness, and her voice was the steady, confident sound I'd grown accustomed to. Julion, Hudson, and Mink were in the room with her, as well. Vance stepped in behind me and closed the door.

"But you—what about—" I couldn't find the words to ask why she was no longer crying in disappointment.

Em laughed and clapped her hands. "Oh, good, I wasn't sure anyone would buy it. I needed an excuse to leave the room immediately and find the guys. We can't let you work for Hooper, right?"

I launched myself on her bed to tackle her in as big of a hug as I could give. She patted my back in a slow, stilted pattern until I released her.

"Sorry," I said, realizing I might have made her uncomfortable.

"Em's not really a hugger," Julion said, smirking and rubbing the cheek she had slapped only days before.

"They gave us an hour," Vance said. "So, if we're making a move, we have to do it right now."

"Are we thinking of some kind of distraction?" I asked.

"Not exactly," Hudson said. "Julion, want to show them what we found out while they were busy downstairs?"

Julion's nostrils flared and he let loose a long, slow breath. "Not really."

"His healing works in reverse!" Hudson exclaimed, sounding far too delighted.

"You can make a healed injury get worse again?" I couldn't piece together what the power would look like in practice.

"I can make a brand-new injury, apparently. Never thought to try it until we were brainstorming up here during the broadcast." Julion glowered at no one in particular.

"My guy!" Vance exclaimed, dropping down to sit on the bed next to Julion and throwing a loose arm over his shoulder. "We just need to get you in contact with an agent, right? Then you can take him down?"

Julion shrugged. "I guess so."

"I'm sorry, Julion, but we need a little more than a 'guess so.'" I cringed as I spoke, hating asking anything of him when he'd so recently thawed toward me. "Sorry," I repeated.

He rolled his eyes. "Yes," he said, then stared right at me. "I solemnly vow my services to attack the agents so you can escape."

I shrunk in on myself, shoulders drooping. He didn't have to be sarcastic about it; I'd already felt bad asking.

"Can you get them both though?" Mink asked in a thoughtful tone. "What if you hurt one, but the other gets the jump on you?"

We were all silent for a moment, mulling over that problem. Earlier in the day, I had wondered about their schedules, when they took breaks, *if* they took breaks. It was too bad we didn't have time to study their moves.

"Em," I said, turning to her.

"Yes?" she asked, lengthening the word while eyeing me narrowly.

"Can you look at the past couple evenings around this time, at what the agents were doing? If they take a break to eat or use the bathroom?"

Em raised her eyebrows and adopted a thoughtful pout. "Not bad, Tallie. Let me check it out."

She performed her patterned breathing and sank into a restful state. Vance leaned forward from where he sat next to Julion and held one of my hands in both of his, rubbing his thumb over the base of my palm. A shiver ran through me at the tingling that lingered in the wake of his touch.

"We need to move soon," Em said, popping her eyes open suddenly enough that Mink and I both jumped. "One agent has been leaving for about fifteen minutes, then the other goes. It happens right around this time. If we want to deal with one at a time, this is our chance."

"We have to," Vance agreed, looking at me for my approval.

"It's mostly up to Julion," I said. "He's the one who has to basically attack one of them."

"Please," Julion scoffed. "Like I haven't been dying to do that all along."

My mind flashed to when he balked at showing off his newfound skill. When Vance hit him, he didn't strike back. His bravado rang false, but it wasn't my place to call him on it. I understood pretending at bravery and hoping it would stick. I understood that all too well.

"Where are we going?" Mink asked.

"We can just go home," Hudson replied. "Em said the rest of us are free to go. It's Vance and Tallie who need to be on the run."

Mink reared his head back, regarding Hudson like he had developed a rotten stench. Hudson chuckled lightly and pulled Mink in to cuddle close to his side.

"Just pointing out the options. We're obviously with you guys. All the way, wherever you need to go to escape Hooper."

My heart considered bursting into a spray of fireworks. They would all be loyal to Vance; they'd run in the same crew forever. But they included *me* in this show of support, and I wanted to cry at how unexpectedly wonderful it felt amid all the heartache.

"Guys, you're going to make Tallie bawl, and we don't have time for that nonsense," Em deadpanned.

"Let me go first on my own," Julion said. "Come down the stairs partway, but don't show yourselves until I, uh, incapacitate this guy."

The urge to cry was swallowed up by the enormity of my nerves. The guys all ran to their own rooms to grab coats and whatever else they wanted to carry on the run.

During the brief moment Em and I were alone, I felt the need to clear the air. "I'm sorry if I made you uncomfortable."

Em raised an eyebrow in question as she shrugged her coat on and dragged her hair free from under it.

"Hugging you," I clarified. "I'm sorry, I was just so happy you weren't sad and that you wanted to help." I pretended to be busy looking for a coat in my cardboard box, though I knew it was a flimsy act, and no such coat existed.

"No worries," she said smoothly. "I actually didn't mind. I'm not used to girls wanting to be friends with me, so it took me off guard."

I straightened from the box. I never had many close friends, aside from Vance and his crew. Bryla was my best friend among the Foretolds, and even that relationship was at arms-length.

"Would you want to be friends with me?" I asked in almost a whisper. "Even with Vance, and …"

Em smiled easily. "He wasn't for me, no matter how it went down. No hard feelings—unless you keep bringing it up because that's already getting annoying."

Considering that for only a second, I burst forward to hug her again. She patted my back exactly two times before pulling away.

"All right, all right. Don't make that a habit."

We were laughing together when the guys returned, but neither of us explained ourselves. The comradery was medicinal, easing the nerves that threatened to render me useless. It was no time to freeze. I had to remember; it was time for anger and action.

CHAPTER 29

I tiptoed down the stairs behind Vance, who insisted on being the first one to follow Julion. Em was right behind me, with Hudson and Mink bringing up the rear. The agents had been omnipresent during the competition, and I worried they would somehow know we were crouched on the stairs, preparing to run. Or they would hear five different sets of breathing suspended on the stairway, a surely suspicious noise.

I moved onto the step next to Vance, wanting to hear Julion and the agent better.

"Hey, man, do they pay you extra per frown?" Julion asked. "Or is it a pay cut each time you say a word?"

There was no reply that I could hear, but I wished I could see the agent's face. It had to be only one. Julion wouldn't be dumb enough to talk like that if both agents were there. I didn't think so, anyway.

"At what point are you supposed to intervene here?" he continued. "Like, exactly how far can someone push you before you deploy whatever secret agent shit you know?"

Vance drew an arm around me and looked back to the others. Was he signaling them to get ready to escape, or did he think we'd need to retreat upstairs because Julion was playing with the agent instead of getting the job done? I squeezed my fists tightly, once each, and tried to calm my breathing. It was almost time.

"Top-level restraint," Julion continued. "I'm almost impressed. Most dudes wouldn't stand me being up in their face like this."

The next sound we heard was a low, keening that quickly escalated to a higher and higher pitch. Vance dropped his arm from my back and bolted to the bottom of the stairs. After a frozen second, he looked back, face grim, and beckoned us down.

Though my attention was mostly on the door, and getting out of it as quickly as possible, I couldn't help staring at the agent.

Julion crouched next to him, where he lay curled on the floor. A series of burns and deep lacerations ran up his exposed arm. His sleeves were pushed up as far as they could go, giving Julion's hands more access to the man's skin, and the wounds disappeared under the fabric. I couldn't see how far they spread, but redness appeared above the agent's collar, circling his neck quickly. Bile rose in my throat, and I turned my attention back to the door.

Mink ran out first. I could barely make out his form in the fading, dusky light as he peered up and down the street before running back to tell us it was clear. Vance took my hand and we left together with the others right behind. I turned around as the door swung shut to see Julion stand from the agent's writhing form and bring up the rear. None of our group would be left behind to face the consequences when the second agent returned from his break to find an injured colleague.

We stood in a tense, jumpy huddle on the sidewalk.

"We never actually decided where to go," Hudson pointed out.

"There are about five minutes left before the other guy shows up from his break," Em said, matter-of-fact. She was the only one who hadn't swiveled her head to scan our surroundings.

"My old house," I said. "My parents aren't—there's no one to put in danger if the agents track us there."

Vance pressed his lips together tightly before nodding once. "It'll work for now."

I turned to lead the way but froze when the distant sound of a familiar engine reached my ears. "Hooper," I breathed.

"Shit," Hudson said, a little too loudly. "They're early. Julion could you—"

Mink cut him off. "Behind the building guys, let's go!"

The six of us ran through the grass and around the building, where we wouldn't be immediately visible from the street.

Unfortunately, we hadn't known that this was where the second agent was taking his break.

He stood from an old folding chair the second we appeared and reached inside his suit jacket.

"What are you doing eating lunch outside in *this* kind of weather?" Hudson asked, oozing confusion and judgment into his tone.

The agent bit. I couldn't believe it. With his hand still in his suit jacket and his lip curled up on one side, he stepped from underneath a tree to stare at the sky, where the first star of the night winked back at him from a cloudless expanse.

In the moment of distraction, Em ran straight at him. No fear, just guts. I wanted to be her if I ever got a chance to finish growing up. She grabbed his arm that had been reaching for what I assumed was a weapon. With both hands, she tugged, her muscles straining.

"Watch out!" I screamed as I saw the agent rear back his other hand to strike her.

Vance was there a second later to block his arm.

Julion was just behind him. "Let go of him," he instructed our friends in a low voice that left no room for argument.

Vance tugged on Em's arm, and they backed up to where I stood with Hudson and Mink.

Julion shot a hand forward to touch the agent's neck. His face paled as the spot under Julion's hand grew blisteringly red, then split open. Deep. Julion moved his hand up just in time to avoid being touched by the blood and pus that started to leak from the wound. The man's eyes rolled back in his head, and he dropped to the ground.

Trying not to reveal my disgust and horror at the move that probably saved our escape, I stared around the back yard. It was fenced on the rear and the sides with solid panels.

Vance's lips touched the outer rim of my ear. "Remember when we dumped all those leaves on Mr. Edmund's yard?"

The man was a notorious grouch in Vance's neighborhood. He prided himself on a pristine lawn, all grass with no trees, flowers, bushes, anything else—a holdover from a couple of generations ago, if my grandparents were to be believed. He also was known for assaulting any stray dogs or people who walked on his property. Along with Vance's crew, we had gathered up as many fallen leaves from every house in the neighborhood that would allow us to rake for them. We put ten lawns worth of fall leaves in his backyard, so they stood knee-high. Of course, Mr. Edmund came outside and caught us before we could run. Vance hoisted me up to stand on his shoulders so I could climb over the fence, and everyone took turns with various circus-level acrobatics until we had all made it safely over.

We were old pros at this.

I mustered a grin for Vance and ran for the rear fence, the others following after. Vance crouched down for me, but I motioned for Em to go first. She hadn't done this with us before, and I wanted to be sure she could make it over. The car engine we had heard in the distance came to rest in front of the dormitory. We were out of time.

I watched nervously as Em grappled with swinging her leg over the top of the fence. Before she made it, I found myself being thrust upward in the air, large hands under my thighs. I looked down to see Julion had taken it upon himself to lift me to the top of the fence. I caught the top and strained to pull myself over. It was taller than Mr. Edmund's fence had been. Em and I dropped down to the other side at the same time. I crumbled on the ground in a heap of my limbs, cringing at the ache from impact. Somehow, Em had landed on her feet with her knees bent and arms out. She reached down a hand to pull me to my feet as Mink and Hudson joined us.

Julion came over the fence next but didn't drop down. Hudson and Mink stood and supported him from below, so he could lean over the fence to grab Vance's hands and hoist him up. The guys all landed in a pile, but everyone stood from it, seemingly unbroken. We were in the backyard of a single-story house that was only fenced in the rear. We could see straight through all of the backyards in a row.

"Left, guys, come on," I said, working out which direction to take to my old house.

"Stay in the backyards?" Vance asked the group, and his question received a chorus of agreement.

We didn't know if anyone saw us jump the fence or not. We didn't know if agents would be stalking the neighborhood, trying to find us. So, we stayed behind houses, sprinting when we had to cross streets, and jogging the rest of the time, to conserve energy. My house wasn't close, by any estimation.

The sky was pitch black. Night had fully descended, and with the cloud cover, not even a lone star was there to guide our way. The street lamps hadn't been functional since I was a little kid. They went away with many other nonessential drains on the available electricity.

The darkness was to our benefit, as the agents would have a harder time spotting us. But navigating yards and curbs and other obstacles proved a little tricky. Vance caught my arm as I stumbled over yet another ball left out for the night in a backyard. If he hadn't been jogging by my side, I would've been on the ground more often than I was up and moving.

Em, who was running at the front of our convoy with directions from me, stopped and motioned for us to halt, as well. I gratefully took the opportunity to catch my breath.

"Does anyone else," Em said through heavy breaths, "think it's weird that we haven't seen any agents or cars out looking for us?"

"Stole the words from me," Hudson panted. "How much longer to your house, Tallie?"

I couldn't answer. I had caught my breath enough to speak, but I couldn't think of the words to confess I was lost. The area around the competition house was not familiar to me. I knew we started out in the right direction for my house. But the further we got, using backyards, not seeing street names, with everything dark, I got twisted. I didn't know where we were or where my house was. The others should have left me behind if I couldn't be any help. The feeling of failure crept through me. I couldn't make it to my own home. How did I expect to do anything right?

"Maybe six blocks that way," Vance said, pointing straight ahead.

"How do you know where my house is?" I asked, shaking out of my self-reproaching thoughts.

"Later, guys," Julion said. "Right now, we take advantage of them not hunting us down."

I nodded, pressing my lips shut. Of course, we didn't have time to unravel the mysteries of Vance's actions during our three years apart. My cheeks burned with embarrassment that I had to be reminded of that.

After another minute of leaning hands on bent knees, calm breathing, and slowing heart rates, we set out again.

Vance was right. He knew exactly where my house was.

It sat dark, as every other house was, with the light curfew in effect. We crept through the neighbors' backyard, then into my own. Past the divination stations my mom had set up for daily practice, leaving no room for any features that would suggest a family had lived here.

I held my breath as I reached for the handle on the back door. My breath whooshed out in a relieved rush when I found it unlocked. I ushered everyone inside, then closed and locked the door behind us. I ran to the front door and locked that as well, then ran around closing blinds and curtains on every window, joined by Mink in doing so. It didn't take long. My parents had chosen to live modestly within our Elite status. The house sat in a neighborhood of Elites but was the smallest for three blocks in every direction.

I pulled the last set of curtains closed and turned toward the darkness of the living room. My memory jumped straight to the details of my parents' deaths, as Em had told them. In this room, they had their last breaths. They bled out, shot to death by the director's men.

Hudson found and lit some candles, passing one to Vance, one to Em, and keeping the third for himself. I jolted my eyes straight up to the ceiling. There had to be stains on the floor, logically I knew that, but I'd at least try to protect myself from confirmation. I blinked rapidly, trying to discourage the welling of my tears. A hand rested on my shoulder, and I jumped, despite the gentle touch.

Vance ran his hand down my arm and slipped it off to rest on my waist.

"Want to get out of this room?" he asked.

I nodded, too consumed to speak. Keeping my eyes trained up and away from the floor, I walked by his side down the hall and to my old bedroom. He closed the door behind us and set the candle on my dresser.

"Wait—I should get everyone else settled. They don't know where anything is," I said, reaching for the doorknob.

Vance shook his head. Strands of his auburn hair gleamed and glinted in mesmerizing waves in the low, flickering light. "They can help themselves. It's fine. You know Hudson, he never goes anywhere without making himself at home."

That earned a short, one-breath chuckle, but I didn't have it in me to truly laugh or smile.

"I wish I had never been Foretold," I whispered, sitting on my bed and scooting back against the headboard. I brought my knees up and wrapped my arms around them, hugging them to my chest.

Vance was quiet for a long time, letting us linger in the echo of my useless wish. Then he crossed the room and sat on the edge of my bed, keeping his feet on the floor. "Why did you laugh when the broadcast said zero Seers died in Arizona?"

There was no leading tone, no suspicion of anything, just regular Vance making regular conversation like we always did.

"Because when I moved the fire, I didn't stop until it showed me an answer of zero."

Vance nodded. "I thought so. Did you change the future?"

He asked it as plainly as anything. He could have asked if I ate oatmeal for breakfast, using that tone. But it didn't shock me as much as it should have, because that same idea had been germinating in the recesses of my mind, not quite ready to sprout.

"Maybe," I admitted.

Vance scooted back on the bed, leaning against the wall. I let go of my knees and stretched out my legs, so they crossed over his. There wasn't anyone else I could have voiced my suspicion to. No one else would have brought it up casually enough to set me at ease.

"Did you know that was possible? Before today?" he asked.

"No. Not at all. If it was something Seers could do, they would get every single person with Seer talent into the Oracus and trained properly." I shook my head, over and over, as I considered the ramifications if *anyone* performing divination could shape the future to their liking. "No, it had to be a coincidence that the result was zero. I mean, you wrote that answer, too, are we sure *you* aren't the one changing the future?"

"Pretty sure," Vance laughed lightly. "I didn't even look at the flames."

I sighed. Predicting the future the regular way had been almost too much pressure for me to handle. If I could shape the future as well … I would collapse under the weight of the mere thought. That much responsibility shouldn't belong to anybody, least of all me.

CHAPTER 30

I fell asleep in my old bed, my head resting in the dip between Vance's shoulder and chest, and one of my legs draped over his. He must have woken before me because as soon as I stirred, he dropped a kiss on my head. I tilted my chin to smile up at him, and he leaned in to kiss my lips.

I recoiled. "Stop, I have morning breath," I protested, turning my head.

My human pillow rumbled beneath me as he chuckled lightly. With gentle fingers, he caught my chin and turned my face back to his. "I want your stale, sleepy, warm, perfect mouth on mine."

He pressed his lips to mine, and thoughts of toothpaste faded almost instantly. There was something different about this kiss. It could have been the setting. I had never kissed anyone in my bed before. It could have been how insulated from any outside dangers I felt, the warmth of our bodies trapped beneath my comforter. It could have been the relief of making it here, safely, away from the dormitory, and away from the agents.

The reason didn't matter. What mattered was how long and deep his kisses ran, the perfect pressure of his grip on my upper arms. The way Vance kissed me that morning held a path forward. He knew it, I knew it, and there was no rush. He took his time to appreciate and cherish each meeting of our lips, each glance of a finger along my skin, lighting up a whole network of sensations inside me.

He pulled his face from mine, and before I could protest, he pulled me into an embrace. I tucked my face into the crook of his neck and inhaled deeply, not caring if he noticed. It was so easy there, in his arms, without any pressure, any demands, threats, or reminders of the recent past. Staying there was all I wanted—which was why we needed to get up, join the others, and make a plan before I lost all concept of the time for anger and action.

I pulled away from him and gasped at the expression on his face. His eyes were wide open and speaking volumes of tenderness. He ran his tongue swiftly across his upper lip. His cheeks were flushed, so full of life and wonder; I had the strangest urge to cry. Then he reached his head forward to kiss me again, and I lost track of any thoughts remaining in my head that weren't *Vance*.

I loved him.

"You see? I'm telling you; the curtains weren't closed yesterday." The words came from outside.

Vance's fingers tensed, digging into my hips. I might have stopped breathing.

"You want to go all the way to headquarters to report curtains?" a second voice said.

"The broadcast said to report any sign," the first voice retorted.

Wordlessly, I slipped out of bed. Vance and I ran to the living room.

Focused on warning the others that people were on the lookout for us, I forgot what sight would await me. I screeched to a halt in the doorway, keeping my eyes up, hating what I might see illuminated in the daylight that peeked around the edges of the curtains. Hooper had never moved my parents to a new home. They had died here, in this spot, bleeding out until a couple of unfeeling men in suits tossed their bodies into a lake.

I brought a hand up to my cheek and felt the tears that I hadn't noticed forming. I shouldn't, I couldn't, there wasn't time. There was something we were supposed to be doing. There was a reason I came into this miserable room. I just couldn't think of what it was. I couldn't think at all.

Voices faded in the background of my rushing, roaring ears, barely audible over the beating of my heart. My body jolted. Someone had me by the shoulders. They gave me another rough shake.

"Tallie, come *on*," Em's normally dry tone broke through my fog with its frantic insistence.

I squeezed my eyes shut as hard as I could. When I opened them, Em's face was almost on top of mine, staring at me with severe planes, casting hard shadows on her pretty face. I nodded, my movement wooden. We had to go. The floor snuck its way into my field of vision, the old sheet vinyl patterned to look like tile. Without a single stain.

My eyes darted around the room then. Em had been so certain in reading my parents' past, but there was no evidence to support they'd been shot here.

"Em, are you positive you saw it happen … here?" I asked.

Mink brushed my hand with gentle fingers, catching my attention, and nodded to a bucket, a pile of sponges, and a mop in the corner of the room. I turned to pull him into a hug, amazed that my old friend would still care enough to do that when he should have been resting.

"It was their idea," he said, pointing first at Em, then at Julion.

Julion?

"We have to leave. Now," Julion said quickly from his position at the window. "Those people are gone."

"Daylight isn't ideal, is it?" Hudson mused, mostly to himself.

"We have to get out of this neighborhood. Nowhere Elites will be," Vance said. "I'm guessing Hooper put out a public directive to turn us in."

I had to come up with an idea, contribute *something* to keep my place with them, to not become dead weight.

"We're too obvious in a big group," I said, my shaky voice breaking more than once. "Should we split up?"

The room went quiet.

"It's a good point," Julion conceded. "Break off into pairs, meet at our spot?"

I had no clue what spot he meant, but Vance, Hudson, and Mink all nodded. The pairs came out naturally. Hudson and Mink were inseparable under any conditions. Vance grabbed my hand and tugged me close to him. That left Julion and Em together. They left the house first, heading left. Hudson and Mink went right. Vance held back in the house with me, stealing a short moment.

"Tallie," he said, taking his time with my name, even when we should have been rushing. "We'll get somewhere safe. Pedestrians won't turn us in, not a chance."

I stared up, wide-eyed at him. Pedestrians weren't fans of Elites or Foretolds, like me. I'd learned that much during the competition.

"Trust that we'll be safe," he continued. "I'm highly motivated to finish what we started."

A surprised laugh broke out of me, but I stuffed it back down quickly as we fled my home. I didn't know if I would see it again.

CHAPTER 31

A block away from my house, Vance slowed his pace. I tugged at his hand, looking at him in question.

"Running will attract attention," he explained. "Most people won't recognize us, so we need to not catch their eye or be memorable."

It made sense, but my legs argued with me, desperate and itching to run until we reached whatever safe haven the group had agreed on.

"Where's the spot?" I asked, inching close to Vance until he wrapped his arm around my back, tucking me into his side as we forced ourselves to stroll.

"Do you remember the mall?"

The city had two different abandoned shopping malls, on opposite sides of the outskirts. Looking at them these days, it was hard to imagine what history had told us, that the different sections used to hold stores full of countless options, unnecessary things to spend money on, use a couple of times, then throw away. Now, as they had been for my whole life, they stood empty and abandoned. Anyone could enter the shells of the stores, as the large front windows were almost all broken out.

Vance noticed my quiet recall and shook his head. "Not those. The Cave."

"The *underground* mall?"

Vance nodded.

"Isn't it kind of dangerous there?" I realized that being out in the open where agents, or people hoping to gain the government's favor could spot us was the most dangerous of all. But the Cave still starred in a few of my nightmares.

Vance and his crew had wanted to check it out one day that I had visited them. We were all about 14. They'd said someone's older cousin told them about this underground mall called the Cave. The few stores it held went out of business before the states separated— before any of the wars. We had searched the neighborhood it was rumored to be in until we found a broken, crumbling brick building with graffiti covering the remnants of its walls. A back section of the building stood untouched; its steel door propped slightly ajar. We'd entered to find a staircase leading down to a long stretch of a wide, grand hallway. In the dim, filtered, dusty light that came down the stairs with us, we found large, tacky furnishings. Over-sized models of airplanes hung from the ceiling. Brightly painted, life-size statues of clowns and fairytale creatures lined the hallway. A large carousel filled the center of the hall farther down. The stores were all dark, but a few lightbulbs along the hall flickered in and out, allowing us to get the full sense of the place.

Vance had cheered and almost immediately dropped his skateboard to the tiled floor and jumped on to ride the length of the hall. Julion and Hudson were right after him, but Mink stood back with me, knowing I didn't skateboard. We'd laughed and teased the guys as they tried various tricks on their boards, but movement in one of the stores had caught my eye. It came closer; a dirty, haggard grown-up. More showed up, coming out of what seemed like every shadow and nook of the place. They had glazed eyes, moved in unsettling, jerky ways, and had quickly advanced on us. Terrified, we had fled the place, taking stairs two at a time up to the surface, and we never went back or talked about it again in the time that I had spent with them.

"We went back a couple years later," Vance said. "There weren't as many people camped out there, and we um, we kind of cleared the place out."

I didn't miss his glossing over the details of *how* they'd cleared it out. But I wasn't so wrapped up in him that I didn't notice a face staring at us, wide-eyed from the window of a house we were passing.

Even though I knew we were trying to look casual, I upped my pace, urging Vance along with me. My head was on a swivel, checking the houses around, seeing if anyone else was on the lookout for us. Curtains twitched in the next house over, but by the time I focused on the window, there was no one there. A car engine revved in a driveway, two houses away from us. It backed out onto the street and sped away, faster than someone should have gone in a neighborhood like this.

No one had confronted us, though, so we continued walking.

Vance picked up the conversation again. "We cleaned the place up some, the hallway at least, and it became our regular hangout. We'd skateboard, ride bikes, hang out, you know."

I nodded, trying to imagine the place without the scary crowd and heaps of litter. It had a somewhat eclectic appeal. I wished I could have been there with them during the missing years. For that's what those three years had been. Missing out on Vance. His arm around me, his voice that alternately soothed and excited me. The way he made me feel so important and special, just for being me. He'd never cared one way or another if I was accomplished as a Foretold, and that was a level of acceptance I had been without for years and years before I met him. More so in the three years without him.

My heart clenched, almost painfully, in a sudden wave of gratitude. That I'd met him back then, and that we'd found each other again. I stopped walking and craned my head around, ensuring no one was around or paying special attention to us. My hands snaked up around Vance's neck, almost on their own, independent of any conscious thought I had. I rose onto my toes and kissed him. His arms wound around me almost instantly, and we savored that moment, lost in the soft and sweet press of lips. I pulled back with a small smile, regretting that we had to keep moving.

The roar of an engine at the far end of the street startled us out of our bubble. It wasn't Hooper's car, but it looked so similar, it had to contain agents.

"Run." Vance's face paled, setting his freckles starkly bold. "If we split up, they can't follow us both."

"What?" I yelled. "We're not splitting up!"

"Keep going until you get to my neighborhood. If I don't catch up right away, tell anyone you know my family. They'll take care of you."

A small, stiff paper was stuffed into my hand.

Vance repeated his instruction. "Run! We have to separate, or they'll catch us. It's our only chance. Backyards only. Go."

My heart hammered wildly in my chest, fear radiating through me with every pump. I trusted Vance. He always kept a clear head. If he said we needed to split up, it had to be the best chance for us to get away. I sprinted in a diagonal, across the yard of a house, then booked it through a series of backyards.

My eyes couldn't concentrate on what was ahead of me. They stole glance after frantic glance across the street. I couldn't see Vance in the gaps between houses, but I had to trust he was running, same as me.

A squeal of brakes came from behind, maybe a block away.

"Where is she?" an unfamiliar voice called out, loud and demanding.

They were coming after us on foot. I doubled down on my speed, pushing my legs to their absolute limit. Then a sharp sound cracked and echoed between the houses. It stopped me faster than a brick wall. Unable to help myself, I crept around the side of a house. I stepped just past the side wall, into the front yard.

I was wrong about the distance. They were two blocks behind me. Two agents stood in the middle of the street, one holding a gun, both staring down at the pavement before them; at the body lying prone and still, capped by the most beautiful auburn hair I had ever seen.

CHAPTER 32

The sob burned its way from my chest all the way up my throat, searing and charring my insides before it burst out of me. I shoved my hands over my mouth, trying desperately to muffle the sound as I backed up, out of their sight.

I had just gotten Vance back. We hadn't had enough time. Not enough at all for him to know how completely my soul belonged to him, how I had never stopped loving him, not for one second, no matter how hard I had tried during those three years. Tears blurred my vision, and I didn't bother blinking them away. I knew they'd be replaced quickly. Endlessly, as I would spend my life mourning Vance, my parents, Ethyl, and soon Gina.

On trembling legs, I stumbled across the yard I was in until I reached the next. I braced my arm against the back wall of a house and leaned forward just in time to vomit on the grass, instead of down the front of my only shirt. Choking and heaving, I emptied what little was in my stomach, then retched with dry heaves until the muscles in my stomach and chest burned and screamed. If I had the luxury of being loud, I would have screamed back at my muscles, that they didn't know the meaning of pain.

I pushed off the house, barely keeping my feet under me. Arms as rigid as steel banded around my chest, tightly enough that it was a struggle to take a breath. I hadn't made it three steps.

"I got her!" an agent called from behind me.

A car rumbled to a halt nearby. The agent lifted me from the ground, and I twisted my body within his grasp, flailing my legs, hoping to land a kick against him.

It was wasted effort. A second agent gripped my ankles, and I was immobilized between the strength of the two men. They shoved me into the backseat of the car, bashing my shoulder on the door frame. It was empty. No Director Hooper. I would have loved nothing more than the chance to hurt him, make him feel even the smallest fraction of what he had inflicted on me. The unfathomable losses he had caused.

A lump caught in my throat as I wondered if Vance's body was in the trunk of the car, inches away from me, separated only by the frame and cushions of the backseat. If not, they had left him bloody and discarded in the middle of the street. I doubled over in my grief, knowing there was no proper place for his body to be unless it was standing, alive, coursing with blood and vitality, and everything good there was in the world. Vance was gone.

A scream tore its way out of me, and I lunged between the front seats. My hands were everywhere, landing as many hits as I could on the agents. I wished I was stronger. I wished I had Julion's power to harm. I would have killed them if I had the means.

The agent in the driver's seat slipped out of the car, so I focused my rage on the other. He tried to capture my wrists, but he couldn't anticipate my wild strikes. I barely noticed the door opening behind me. A blunt pain crashed against the side of my face, then I knew nothing but the constraint of oblivion.

***

White walls surrounded me. The bed beneath me was as solid and unyielding as the street I had last seen Vance lying on. I tried to sit up, but my head swam with the motion. I laid my head back down and instead turned it slowly to the side, trying to figure out where I was.

Even that small movement made my head swim. I tried to bring my hand up to rub my forehead but resistance against my wrist wouldn't allow the movement. I tried my other hand, but it was strapped in place at the side of the bed, too. My heart rate picked up, then my breathing. I couldn't move. Trapped. I sucked in air; too much, too fast, over and over.

Dark spots appeared at the edges of my vision, crowding in on the light. I closed my eyes, trying to focus on my breathing first. Panicking wouldn't help. This was a bad dream. I was asleep in bed at my old home, cuddled against Vance. I would wake up soon, and we would pick up where we left off. This time, we wouldn't be interrupted, because the director hadn't put out a broadcast instructing people to report any sightings of us. We would be free to live together, to be whoever we wanted to be, away from any pressure or influence, or murderous agents.

As desperately as my heart wanted that to be true, I knew it was a delusion. The fantasy of a broken mind.

In reality, I knew I had reached my years-long goal; the only thing I ever thought I was meant for. I was inside the Oracus.

TO BE CONTINUED IN BOOK 2

ACKNOWLEDGMENTS

This is my first fully self-published novel, and man is it ever nerve-wracking to be the lone responsible party. The help I've received from others along the way has been invaluable and I am deeply grateful for everyone who helped get this novel to its final form.

Thank you to Jai Design for the original cover art.

Thank you to Black Quill Editing, and I swear that any errors found within the book are due to my own stubborn style choices and are not their influence!

Thank you especially to my early readers, notably Amy, Meghan, Megan, Cassie, and of course, my mom! If your name isn't listed here, it's only because I'm terribly disorganized and searched and searched my inboxes for everyone who beta read and couldn't find the … evidence? I appreciate you so much!!!

Thank you to Green Elk Publishing for taking on my first published novels, giving me the confidence to pursue a career in writing that I might never have found otherwise.

Thank you to Brenda Peregrine who gave me an amazing crash course in story crafting when I brought her onboard for book coaching on an early, early project of mine. Her expertise and friendship was so greatly appreciated, and I'm not sure I would've continued on writing other stories without that boost.

Thank you to my family for being supportive of my fiction habit. It doesn't appear to be resolving any time soon.

And an ETERNAL thanks to everyone reading this. I swear, you are the things my dreams are made of—in the least creepy way possible!

ABOUT THE AUTHOR

Corrie Hathaway is the author of the Young Adult fantasy trilogy, Through Smoke and Sand. She is a former RN, a mom, a wife, a cat person, a Midwesterner who longs for the Pacific Northwest, an awkward soul, a compulsive over-smiler, and a lifelong reader who is deeply grateful for all the fictional escapes that have seen her through life.